THE FREE EAGLES

FOUNDATION AND ADVENTURES

DEV

Made with ❤ on the Notion Press Platform
www.notionpress.com

I dedicate this book to my friend ansh.

Contents

CHAPTER ONE

The Foundation of the Free Eagles

In the year 2019, A boy Dev who was 9 years old at that time moved to a new city Meerut. His father was an army officer. His family was living in Deotrant Enclave. Dev was a confident kid but he was an introvert that's why he has very less friends. On the other hand in Jammu & Kashmir there was a boy ansh. His father was also an army officer. He was very extroverted and he will take any challenge like any bicycle stunt or going to a strange place in night without the permission of his parents. Then a year passed by and now he and his family had to moved to a new station. They moved to meerut and then they searched for a house and they find one in the Deotrant Enclave. They moved to Deotrant Enclave. After some days a new boy came to the park he was none other than ansh everybody was staring at him then one boy came to him and asked his name. He said my name is ansh and what is your's the other boy said my name is dev. At that day they became friends. They play cricket together, they play football together but the most that they love to do is cycling. They both called themselves legendary riders. Then they think how cool is this that can they make a secret goup. Then the process of making a secret group began: Ansh and Dev think about many names like Legendary Cyclers, Two Legends, Cool Boys and many more. After thinking many names Dev told ansh that they will come tomorrow at 11:00 AM and then think about the name of their group. At night in his home ansh searched many names on the internet for a secret group but he find nothing. Then he saw a eagle made of steel and stitched to a piece of cloth and in above of that eagle was written Free Eagles. Actually that was his father old badge on which the unit name in which his father worked earlier was written and then he had idea that they could take this name for their secret group name. Next day Ansh presented this idea to Dev and Dev also liked this idea and Ansh has given Dev the badge of free eagles. Ansh also created a password for the Free Eagles so that he could know that he was Dev only not any other person. The password is Shut it down and the headquarter of free eagles is Ansh's House. Ansh also tell Dev that the work of the Free Eagles is to face any challenge that is difficult to do and unlock new mysteries in their city.

CHAPTER TWO

The Origins

Ansh and Dev meet after making their group. Dev we have maken our group but we don't know our origins we don't know when we are born and what have we done in life so far, Firstly dev you tell me. Ok, I was born in the year 2010 on 19 september. I was born in Bihar. I was a brilliant child. I always got great marks in school. At the age of nine I was a great fan of science. I just loved science and my inspiration was one of the greatest scientist of all time Nikola Tesla. I always watch science and science experiment videos. I had also participated in science exhibition and has done many science experiment like a model of mars rover and a drone. After that when I was ten years old I was attracted to cricket a sports played with bat and ball. I gets coaching of professional cricket and I also has interest in coding, so I had learned java and maken many apps and games like a basketball game and a soccer game. I have also written and published my own book How to start your own business? which is available online. Now you tell me your story? I was born on 28 february 2012. I was born in Delhi. I am a average child in school and i loved art from my childhood. I have maken many drawings and also winned many competition in my school and i am also expert in taekwondo in which i have brown belt. Ok so now we know our origins so let's walk and talk and play truth and dare. Stone,Paper,Scissor I win! what will you choose ansh truth or dare. I will choose truth. Ok my question is did you ever has stolen anything in your life? Yes, i stole biscuits from the drawer. Ok Stone,Paper,Scissor I win! what will you choose dev truth or dare? I will choose truth. Did you ever ring the bell of your neighbour and ran away. Yes, i did. This will be last after that we will go home Stone,Paper,Scissor Yes, I win again! Ha Ha Ha! What will you choose dev now truth or dare? I will choose truth. Ok, Now i will ask the same question that you had asked me did you ever stole anything in your life? Actually no, i did't stole anything in my life. So now its time to go home bye bye.

CHAPTER THREE

Shourya Mahika and more

On the next day, they have a meeting in ansh's house. Dev what about the children in this enclave can we take anyone in our group. We will discuss each of them now in the meeting but first can you make some popcorn for me. Ofcourse you just wait 5 minutes. After 5 minutes here is your popcorn so now we start our discussion so the first child is Shourya and you know how bad he is he bully children in school. He also spoke bad words about our mother and father so we could not include him in our group. Next is Mahika i think she is a good girl so we should include her in our group. No, never you don't know dev how bad she is she always argue with me without any reason. If i ask her any question she starts to argue with me. She always spoke bad about me in front of others and tell others that i am very bad because of her others think bad about me. I will never accept her in our group. Ok no problem we will not include her in our group. Ok so before we talk about another child can you bring me some drinks. There is your drinks and here we go so the next child is Rishu or Rithwik or what you call him doesn't matter can we include him in our group. What's your point about him?

I think we should not keep him in our team because he can't keep any secret. Whenever i tell him a secret the next day he tell everyone about my secret and the second problem is he gets hyper very quickly i you tell him a joke about him he will get angry and try to beat you so i will tell the next so can we pick your sister dev in our group. Actually, no we can't keep her because she also can't keep any secret and she will argue with you without any reason. She will slap you without any reason. That's why we can't keep her in our group. Ok what about Reeyansh he is a good boy. He always keep any secret that we tell him and he also didn't argue with you without any reason or never slap you without any reason or never bully anyone in school. Actually, he is very young to join our group. He is still a small kid that cannot go to any missions or challenges that we will face. Ok last but not the least Dev what about aadhya. She always keep any secret that we tell her and she also will not argue with you without any reason or never slap you without any reason or never bully anyone and she is also not too young. Ok we will talk with her in the evening but for now let's enjoy popcorn and drinks. After some time. Ok ansh i am leaving now and i will come in the evening and we will talk with her. In the evening, Ting-Tong I think it would be probably ansh. Hello ansh whats up. Did you forget we have to talk to aadhya about the joining of our group. Yes ok let's go. Hi aadhya. Hello. We have to talk to you that if you can join our group Freeeagles. What will you do in your group. Actually, we will go to missions and adventures that we will face in our future. Could you join us? Actually, my mother would not allow me to go out of this enclave alone so i am sorry! Can't you convince your mother about joining of our group. No i can't because she is very strict so i am sorry! Ok no problem .

So now we two will be the only two boys in our group. Ok now let's play and on the next day we will search for anyone who wants to join our group in the BC Joshi enclave and if anyone is willing to join then we will consider him or her and then we will decide that he or she can come in our group. On next day, ok so dev we have 5 children who wants to join our group. So we will create posts for them. I and you we both have captain post in our group and the children who will join us will get a post name manager in our group. Their work is to manage our headquarter and give information about what's going on in both the enclaves. Ok fine, let's start so the first child is ronik, so with the information that i collected about him with his sister and his friends. It seems like he is not good enough to join our group as a manager because his friends telled me that he is very careless and he did not take anything seriously. So what your comment on that dev? I think you are right because we cannot take a careless person in our group. Ok, the next child is arnav and what can i say about him because he has everything that we don't need in our group. He is a careless person, he play video games entire day and he is also very lazy and we can't keep this type of people in our group.The next child is tanvi actually she is very good girl. She always tops in her school and she is also very hardworking and passonate about working in a group but the problem is she is very young to get in our group. Get me some water ansh. Ok, here is your water and now you will tell me the next child. Ok, now we have aryan. He is very responsible child and he also works hard and he also score good marks in his school and he is also now too young and he is independent as well. This is my boy wooooo! he will become the manager of our group. One minute ansh we haven't discussed the last child and the last child is anil and we can't make him the manager of our group because again he is very lazy and careless. So final our manager will be aryan. Let's talk to him in today's evening. In the evening, ting-tong . Hello! i think you both are dev and ansh so if i am guessing right you have selected me for manager in the freeeagles. Yes you are right . You are the first manager of the freeeagles. Would you be able to manage our headquarter anytime . Yes i would. Ok in the first month we will observe your work and then we will give you your salary accordingly. After observing from the next month we will give you $10 or as much as $100 per month. Deal yes deal. Ok come from the next day. Ok dev now we have getted our manager for our group so now let's play.

CHAPTER FOUR

Mission: The Mall

After forming the group Free Eagles and finding their manager. They have told everybody that they have a group named Free Eagles and they could face any challenge . Shourya thought that this is good oppourtunity earn money. So he had given him challenge that can they spend a night at the Ghostly bungalaw outside the city named as The Mall and if theycan then he will give him $100 and if they can't then they have to give him $100. Ansh has accepted his challenge but Dev was little frightened that what if they could find a real ghost at The Mall but Ansh told him there is no such thing like ghosts in this world. Shourya has also told them to record that they were going to The Mall and spending the night at The mall. The month is of April and today is 2nd April and you have to go in the night of 3rd april. I think dev we will go with bicycles and we will take a phone for finding the route to the mall through GPS and we will also take some woods and a matchstick to burn fire there, a torch, some food and water and a tent to sleep there. Days and night passed and came the night of 3rd april at 10 o clock when dev's parents slept he slipt out of his house with phone and torch and after some time ansh also comed with the woods, matchstick, camera and a tent which can be fold in his bag. Dev can you call aryan so that we can inform him that we are going on a mission. Ok hello! aryan Hi! dev ok aryan we are going on a mission on the mall in the outskirts of the cith so i have just called you to inform you about that ok good luck.Ok so now we go and dev also watch GPS and i am recording on my camera that we are going to The Mall. Finally we reached our destination. The Mall is actually an old bungalaw and was maden britishers 80 or 90 years ago. It is really looking scary at night just look around ansh it has very big bushes around it very old and big trees and it is really a big bungalaw but mostly parts of the bungalaw is in ruins. Ansh i am really frightened and i am also but we have to find a place to pitch our tent. here we can pich our tent.Here is our tent and here we pitched our tent. Ansh it is it is already 12 o clock midnight. Wr have to spent the next 4 to 5 hours in our tent. Ansh record that we are here at. the mall capture everything that is here. Now ansh let's sleep but first i will set a alarm of 5o clock. ding-dong dev wake up it already 5 AM in the morning and now we have to return to our homes and in the evening we will show shourya our recording and will get our $100. In the evening, ansh we have to show shourya the recording. Oh! yes let's go. Here is the recording shourya now give our $100 dollars. Here is your $100.Now, we have became very popular in the Enclaveansh yes bro you are right now we have to take some more challenges. On the next day a boy omi gave them a challenge that can they ride their bicycle with the front tire lifted in the air if they can he will give him $10. Ok so you are sure that you will give us $10. Yes i am sure. Here you go. Let go ansh ye boy. Just watch this omi woooooo! look at this omi this is your stunt that you have told us to do. Now give the $10. Here is your $10 Now we will bought two new vip badge for freeeagles and with the another $5 we will bought a binocular but for now let's go home.

CHAPTER FIVE

Base Alpha: Making

hello! hello! dev yes who? i am ansh ok ansh tell what happened dev i have a crazy idea come to my house i will tell you. Ok i am coming in the evening. Ting-tong hey dev come inside what would you wanna take water or juice. Give me juice. Ok, here is your juice . Ok now tell me what is your crazy idea so dev come oudside. Look at that wall which is in the middle of Deotrant and bc joshi enclave behind that wall there is such a place from where we can watch everything happening in deotrant enclave and bc joshi enclave. So i am thinking that can me built a base there like army. Ok we can but i will take time and a lot of effort. Ok so we are starting the work of building the base from tomorrow morning. Ok so what will we name the base. I think we should name it base alpha. We should make floor with the rocks that are around there and we should not built roof because it will not look nice and takes a lot of effort to built it.We should make our sitting arrangement by dismantling the metal parts of the bench in the park. i will bring my binocular so we can see far away what is happening there and dev you also bring your drone so we can see from above what is happening in both the enclaves. We should also call aryan for building our base. Ok dev. Hello! aryan we have a plan actually we are building our base you know the wall between deotrant enclave and bc joshi enclave. We are building our base alpha there so we need your help so can you come in tommorow morning. Ok. Aryan is coming tomorrow morning so everything is set. ya. Next morning, ya dev you have comed aryan has also comed he is already in the work. Dev you help me to lift this metal piece for our sitting. aaa! yeah so we have maken and setteled our seating. Now time for making our floor so aryan give me that rock. Ok dev aa! yeah ansh give me that rock wo! so our floor is completed now. here will be our binocular stand and here i will keep my drone. So our base is done and dusted now let's do some cycling and aryan you also come with us. Ok so we are legendary riders and he is our new legendary rider. Ok dev, we will start the work of the base tomorrow morning. Ok ansh but for now hail! free eagles!

CHAPTER SIX

Base Alpha: Observing

Dev can you make a flag for base alpha. Ok, i will make the flag in 3-4 days but for now i have drone so let's fly it. Ok give me the remote . So here you go so what is the maximum height that i can fly this drone. You can fly this drone 100 feet above the ground above that remote has no control over the drone. I can see there are two labours who are cutting grass in the bc joshi enclave and there are some children walking and a dog is also there and some cars and bikes. So now i am bringing down the down aa! aa! aa! ya. Just look there there are some people there and their intentions are not looking good. Give me your binocular i will see what are they doing. Aa they are just some labours. Dev listen i am thinking that if anybody in night could come and destroy our base or steal something how do we gonna find that who did that. So i am thinking that could we place a camera at our base and we could watch the recording of the camera live in our phone. Actually ansh we don't have enough budget to place a camera in our base. There are many ideas on internet on how to make camera with old phone but the problem is i don't have a old phone in my house so do you have a old phone in your house. Yes i do. So bring that old phone today's evening and i have the app in my phone from which i can watch the recording live and i will also share the url with you so that you can also watch the live recording so for now let's do cycling and explore what is happening in both the enclaves. So nothing is happening in Deotrant enclave so let's go to BC joshi. Look there dev there are some children fighting. Let's go and know why are they fighting. Hello! kids why are you fighting. We are fighting because he is cheating in the game that we are playing. Ok hey! boy don't do that again. So now dev we will meet in the evening. Bye, Bye. Ansh here is the old phone that you were asking for . On the wifi of that phone. Ok. So i have connected your phone with mine now open the camera of that phone. Opened it. Yes look the footage from the camera of that phone is coming to my phone but there is still one problem how do we charge this old phone. I have a power bank which can run this phone 20 hours and ofcourse i will recharge the phone and the power bank in the morning and then put that back in the evening. That's a good idea so bring your power bank. Wait a minute. Here it is and now where do we place our camera so that anybody could not see it. Ok look we could put our camera in the bushes there and nobody could see it and we could also watch our base. Ok so now we have plced our camera so ansh can you send me the url with which i can see the recording of the camera. Ofcourse. I have send it and now it's very late in the evening so now we should have to go home. Bye,Bye.

CHAPTER SEVEN

Base Alpha: Destruction

Hey dev please bring your drone now it's observation time. Ok i am coming in two minutes. Hello ansh here is your drone and what are we gonna do today. We are gonna observe everybody's roof and seeing that what is in their roof. That sounds like a silly thing but it's fun. So first Shouray's roof. So there are only some iron rods and some pieces of wood there. There are bricks on the roof of mahika and now i am gonna seeing yours. Ooh there is a kite and a cat on your roof.Now i am gonna see rishu's roof so there are some old wood on the roof of rishu. Ok now now we have to stop our observation and do cycling or we can play cricket because the battery of my drone is low so i have to charge it. Ok can you bring bat and ball so that we can play cricket. Ok. First ansh you bat i will bowl and we will play a match of 1 over or 6 balls. Here's first ball. Miss. Here's second ball a couple of runs. third bowl miss. fourth ball that's four! ansh that's a good shot. fifth ball one run. So you have maken 7 runs of 5 balls and now this is the last ball. AAh! four so i have to make 12 runs in one over. Here's is your first ball a single. second ball that's a dot. 2 balls and only one run now you have to make 11 runs in 4 balls. third ball four!. It's 7 in 3.fourth ball a couple 5 in 2. fifth ball that's a miss. Now one ball and five runs you need a six! to win this match. Here comes the last ball and it's aaa four!. It's a tie. Now we have to do super over of three balls. First you bat dev. First ball a couple. Second ball that's a four! and here is third ball it's a six! . So i need 13 in three balls. Here comes your first ball a miss. Second ball four! and here is your third bowl and it's a four!. So you lose by 4 rune and now it's time to go home. Ok dev i will call you the next day about the recording of the camera and i will not come in evening as i am going to a party. Hey! dev that's something strange recorded in our camera there is someone who has comed in night and has destroyed our base. I cannot see the face of that person clearly. Take the screenshot of that person and send it to me i will edit the image and then you can see the face of the person and after that we can ask him why have you done it. Hello ansh i am sending you the image of the perso. Dev they are the kids of servants and i know them. Come to my house. Ok. Hi ansh what are we gonna doing? we are just gonna beat them. No we can't do that we are the kids of officers and what will be the difference between us and them. We are gonna give them warning. Ok let's go. Hey you! me yes you! come here. why have you destroyed our base. Which base i have not destroyed it. Don't lie to me. What is this? you f*****g idiot don't do that again or i will kill you dumb f**k. Calm down ansh. Go away from here. Ok ansh what will we do next. What else we will build our new base.

CHAPTER EIGHT

A new era: the charlie era

Do dev this time we will make a base like an army base. The name of the base will be Charlie. So ansh i will make the blueprint of the base that how will it look and we will also make weapons. To attack on enemies from our base. We will also buy something new for observation. We already have binoculars and drone so what can we buy next for observation. We would buy a telescope to observe stars and moon in the night sky and it's my work. Dev i will buy 1 more camera for our base so that when we are not here we can observe from different angles that what is happening in our base. I have also a plan for making walls of base but there is a wall in front of the base. No i am talking about the side and behind. We could make that wall from sand bags. There are many sandbags in bc joshi. We could use that. So fist task of the day is to make the wall of charlie. Ansh call aryan. Ok, Hey aryan can you come to the location of our old base because we need your help to lift sandbags and make the wall of our new base. Ok, so you guys are building a new base just after your old base got destroyed one day ago. I am coming.Huhhh! done it so we have built our new base wall and now you can go aryan. Ok bye! . What about weapons? Today i will watch video on youtube on how to make homemade weapons and tomorrow i will explain you how to make that weapon. Ok bye! .

Hello ansh! I have three weapon ideas .

First is Paper Crossbow. Second is Cardboard Battle Axe. Third is Duct Tape Nunchucks.

Dev can you make all these three. Yeah but it will take me three days so before that we can order our telescope. So you see and choose telescope and order it. I am going home for making weapons.

3 days later.

Hey ansh here is paper crossbow,Axe and Nunchuks and one additional weapon spear. I have also a thing this telescope. Now we have to place it and i have also found that we will place it in the middle of the base dev. ok sir. Now our telescope is placed and in night we will come and watch stars with the telescope.

CHAPTER NINE

Watching the cosmos with stories

8:30 PM.

Dev when will you come. Ansh said. I am coming. Dev said.

5 minutes later.

hey ansh i habe comed. Let's start the gazing in the cosmos. Dev we will get it turn by turn. First i will watch and you will tell me a story. Let's start. Oh the moon is very beautiful.

So the title of the story is-

"The Curse of Black Lake"

It was a small town, nestled in the heart of the countryside. The people of Black Lake had lived there for generations, and they were proud of their history and traditions. But there was one place in town that they avoided at all costs - the lake.

"The Mysterious Lake"

The lake was said to be cursed, and the townspeople whispered that strange things happened there at night. The water was always black, no matter how sunny the day, and it was said to be bottomless. But despite the rumors, a group of friends decided to take a swim in the lake one summer afternoon.

As they swam, they noticed that the water was warmer than they expected. They also noticed that it was much deeper than they thought, and they soon found themselves being pulled down by a powerful current.

"The Drowned Village"

When they emerged from the water, they found themselves in a village that was entirely underwater. The buildings were overgrown with algae and seaweed, and the air was thick with the stench of decay. The friends realized that they had stumbled upon a drowned village, one that had been lost for centuries.

"The Curse Unveiled"

As they explored the village, they heard strange whispers and moans. They turned to see ghostly figures emerging from the shadows, pointing at them and mouthing silent words. The friends were paralyzed with fear, and they realized that they were in the presence of the curse.

The curse had been cast long ago, by a powerful witch who had been wronged by the villagers. She had drowned the entire village, and the curse had kept it underwater ever since. The friends were now trapped in the village, unable to leave.

"The Escape"

The friends knew that they had to find a way out. They remembered a spell that could break the curse, and they decided to use it. They recited the spell, and the ghostly figures disappeared. The water began to recede, and the friends were able to make their way back to the shore.

But they knew that they had not truly escaped the curse. The drowned village was still there, waiting for its next victims. And the people of Black Lake whispered that the lake was still cursed, and that strange things still happened there at night.

From that day on, the friends were never the same. They had faced the horrors of the drowned village, and they were grateful to have escaped with their lives. But they also knew that the curse was still out there, waiting to claim its next victim. And they warned others never to venture too far into the black waters of Black Lake.

It was a interesting story. Ansh said. Now it's my turn. Dev said. Ok dev i will tell you a story. Ansh i can see the creators on mars.

"The Abandoned Cabin"

It was supposed to be a fun camping trip with friends, but things quickly took a dark turn. The group had decided to hike deep into the woods, to a remote cabin that was rumored to be abandoned.

As they approached the cabin, they realized that it was much older and dilapidated than they had imagined. The windows were boarded up, and the door was hanging off its hinges. But their curiosity got the better of them, and they decided to take a look inside.

As they entered the cabin, they were greeted by a musty, damp smell. The furniture was covered in a thick layer of dust, and cobwebs filled the corners of the room. But the strangest thing was that the cabin appeared to be untouched, as if it had been abandoned in the middle of a normal day.

"The Haunted Study"

One of the friends, a history buff, was drawn to a study in the back of the cabin. The room was filled with old books, maps, and documents. He began to flip through the pages of an ancient tome, when suddenly the room grew cold. The friends heard strange whispers and moans coming from the shadows.

The friend dropped the book and ran out of the room, his face ashen. The others followed him outside, where they huddled together, trying to make sense of what had just happened.

"The Unseen Terror"

That night, as they tried to sleep in their tents, they heard strange noises coming from the woods. Branches snapping, twigs cracking, and the sound of heavy footsteps. The friends were paralyzed with fear, unable to move or speak.

In the morning, they found deep footprints around their tents, but there was no sign of what could have made them. They tried to leave, but the path back was blocked by an unseen force. They were trapped.

"The Final Showdown"

The friends realized that they were dealing with something supernatural, and they needed to act fast. They remembered a story about a protective spell that could keep evil at bay, and they decided to use it.

As they recited the spell, a bright light surrounded them, and the unseen terror retreated. They were able to leave the woods and make their way back to civilization, but they never forgot the horrors that they had faced in the abandoned cabin.

From that day on, they were changed. They knew that there were things in the world that defied explanation, and they were grateful to have escaped with their lives. But they also knew that the evil they had encountered was still out there, waiting for its next opportunity to strike.

Now dev last time i will see and then you. Ok. oh my goodness! saturn's rings are so beautiful.

"The Haunting of Hillcrest Manor"

Hillcrest Manor was a grand estate that had stood for centuries on the outskirts of the town. It was said to be haunted, but the stories were dismissed as mere legends. That was until a group of friends decided to explore the abandoned mansion one dark and stormy night.

"The Eerie Atmosphere"

As they approached the manor, they felt a strange energy in the air. The wind was howling, and the rain was beating down on the roof. The windows were boarded up, and the front door was creaking on its hinges. But their curiosity got the better of them, and they decided to venture inside.

The inside of the mansion was just as eerie as the outside. The walls were peeling, and the furniture was covered in cobwebs. The air was thick with the smell of decay, and the floorboards creaked with every step they took.

"The Ghostly Apparitions"

As they explored the first floor, they heard strange noises coming from the second floor. They decided to investigate, and as they climbed the stairs, they saw ghostly apparitions floating in the air. The friends were terrified, and they turned to run, but they found that the staircase had disappeared.

"The Curse of Hillcrest Manor"

They realized that they were dealing with something supernatural, and they needed to act fast. They remembered a story about a curse that had been placed on the manor centuries ago, by a powerful witch who had been wronged by the residents of the town. The curse had kept the manor abandoned, and it had also trapped the spirits of the dead within its walls.

"The Final Confrontation"

The friends knew that they had to break the curse and free the spirits. They found an old book in the library that contained the spell to break the curse, and they recited it together. The ghostly apparitions disappeared, and the staircase reappeared. The friends were able to escape the mansion and make their way back to safety.

From that day on, Hillcrest Manor was never the same. The curse had been lifted, and the spirits were finally at peace. But the friends were never the same. They had faced the horrors of Hillcrest Manor, and they knew that there were things in the world that defied explanation. And they warned others never to venture too close to the abandoned mansion on the outskirts of town.

Now it's my turn. Dev said. The last story. Ansh Said. Time for jupiter. Dev said.

"The Abandoned Asylum"

There was an old asylum on the outskirts of town that had been abandoned for years. The building was said to be haunted, and the townspeople whispered about strange noises that could be heard coming from within its walls. But despite the rumors, a group of friends decided to explore the asylum one dark and stormy night.

"The Haunted Halls"

As they entered the building, they were immediately struck by the eerie atmosphere. The air was thick with the smell of decay, and the floorboards creaked with every step they took. The walls were peeling, and the windows were boarded up, allowing only a small amount of moonlight to filter in.

The friends explored the first floor, and they soon realized that they were not alone. They heard strange noises coming from the upper floors, and they decided to investigate. As they climbed the stairs, they saw ghostly apparitions floating in the air. The friends were terrified, and they turned to run, but they found that the staircase had disappeared.

"The Cursed Patients"

They realized that they were dealing with something supernatural, and they needed to act fast. They remembered a story about a curse that had been placed on the asylum years ago, by a vengeful spirit that had been wronged by the patients within its walls. The curse had kept the asylum abandoned, and it had also trapped the spirits of the patients within its walls.

"The Desperate Escape"

The friends knew that they had to break the curse and free the spirits. They found an old book in one of the rooms that contained the spell to break the curse, and they recited it together. The ghostly apparitions disappeared, and the staircase reappeared. The friends were able to escape the asylum and make their way back to safety.

From that day on, the abandoned asylum was never the same. The curse had been lifted, and the spirits were finally at peace. But the friends were never the same. They had faced the horrors of the asylum, and they knew that there were things in the world that defied explanation. And they warned others never to venture too close to the abandoned building on the outskirts of town.

So bye ansh. Today we have a lot of fun and i know that you are going posting tomorrow and today is 12 feb and today is hug day. So we have our last hug today. Bye ansh. Have a good year ahead. Dev said. Same to you. Ansh said. And one extra story for you ansh. Dev said.

"Farewell to a Friend"

John and Michael had been best friends since childhood. They grew up together, went to the same school, and even lived in the same neighborhood. But their lives took a different turn when John received a job offer in a different city.

"The Move"

John was excited about the opportunity, but he was also sad to leave his best friend behind. Michael understood John's situation, but he couldn't help but feel a sense of loss. They had been through so much together, and the thought of not seeing each other every day was hard to bear.

Despite their sadness, John made the move to the new city. He was determined to make a success of his new life, and he threw himself into his work. But no matter how busy he was, he never forgot about his best friend back home.

"The Letters"

John and Michael wrote to each other every week. They shared their hopes and fears, and they talked about their dreams for the future. They promised to stay in touch no matter what, and they made plans to visit each other as soon as they could.

Years passed, and John's life in the new city flourished. He had a successful career and a happy family, but he never forgot about his best friend. Michael was still living in their hometown, and he was proud of his friend's achievements.

"The Goodbye"

One day, John received a letter from Michael that would change everything. Michael had been diagnosed with a terminal illness, and he didn't have long to live. John was devastated. He knew that he had to see his friend one last time, so he booked a flight back to their hometown.

When John arrived, he found Michael in a hospice. He was weak, but he smiled when he saw his best friend. They spent the next few days together, talking about old times and reminiscing about their childhood. John promised to take care of Michael's family, and Michael promised to never forget his friend.

"The Farewell"

The day came when Michael passed away. John was at his bedside, holding his hand. He wept as he said goodbye to his best friend, the friend who had been a part of his life for as long as he could remember.

John stayed in their hometown for a few more days, to attend Michael's funeral and to say goodbye to the place that held so many memories for him. As he boarded his plane back to the new city, he felt a sense of loss that he knew would never go away.

Years have passed since John said farewell to his best friend, but he still thinks of Michael every day. He knows that their friendship will never die, and that the memories they shared will always be with him. And he is grateful for the time they had together, the time that will never be forgotten.

The story and chapters end here.

Reality

Actually Freeeagles is a real group made by real best friends dev and ansh but there have been many people who have comed in this group and gone and here are the names of the people { Mahika, Aradhya, Tanvi, Rishu } but these all were not strong enough to face the challenges. I don't want to hurt anyone by this book but what i am saying is truth and i believe that truth cannot hurt anyone and once again i am going to remind you that i dedicate this book to my friend ansh and i am writing this book at a time that after two months in march 2023 he will go to next city. because his posting has come and i want to gift this first part to him and i am going to give tribute to ansh by writing his name 10000 times here: Ansh Ansh Ansh Ansh Ansh Ansh Ansh Ansh Ansh Ansh Ansh Ansh Ansh Ansh Ansh Ansh

Ansh Ansh Ansh Ansh Ansh Ansh Ansh Ansh Ansh Ansh Ansh Ansh Ansh Ansh Ansh Ansh

Ansh Ansh Ansh Ansh Ansh Ansh Ansh Ansh Ansh Ansh Ansh Ansh Ansh Ansh Ansh Ansh

Ansh Ansh Ansh Ansh Ansh Ansh Ansh Ansh Ansh Ansh Ansh Ansh Ansh Ansh Ansh Ansh

Ansh Ansh Ansh Ansh Ansh Ansh Ansh Ansh Ansh Ansh Ansh Ansh Ansh Ansh Ansh Ansh

Ansh Ansh Ansh Ansh Ansh Ansh Ansh Ansh Ansh Ansh Ansh Ansh Ansh Ansh Ansh Ansh

Ansh Ansh Ansh Ansh

Ansh Ansh Ansh Ansh Ansh Ansh Ansh Ansh Ansh Ansh Ansh Ansh Ansh Ansh Ansh Ansh

Ansh Ansh Ansh Ansh Ansh Ansh Ansh Ansh Ansh Ansh Ansh Ansh Ansh Ansh Ansh Ansh

Ansh Ansh Ansh Ansh Ansh Ansh Ansh Ansh Ansh Ansh Ansh Ansh Ansh Ansh Ansh Ansh

Ansh Ansh Ansh Ansh Ansh Ansh Ansh Ansh Ansh Ansh Ansh Ansh Ansh Ansh Ansh Ansh

Ansh Ansh Ansh Ansh Ansh Ansh Ansh Ansh Ansh Ansh Ansh Ansh Ansh Ansh Ansh Ansh

Ansh Ansh Ansh Ansh Ansh Ansh Ansh Ansh Ansh Ansh Ansh Ansh Ansh Ansh Ansh Ansh

Ansh Ansh Ansh Ansh

Ansh Ansh Ansh Ansh Ansh Ansh Ansh Ansh Ansh Ansh Ansh Ansh Ansh Ansh Ansh Ansh

Ansh Ansh Ansh Ansh Ansh Ansh Ansh Ansh Ansh Ansh Ansh Ansh Ansh Ansh Ansh Ansh

Ansh Ansh Ansh Ansh Ansh Ansh Ansh Ansh Ansh Ansh Ansh Ansh Ansh Ansh Ansh Ansh

Ansh Ansh Ansh Ansh Ansh Ansh Ansh Ansh Ansh Ansh Ansh Ansh Ansh Ansh Ansh Ansh

Ansh Ansh Ansh Ansh Ansh Ansh Ansh Ansh Ansh Ansh Ansh Ansh Ansh Ansh Ansh Ansh

Ansh Ansh Ansh Ansh Ansh Ansh Ansh Ansh Ansh Ansh Ansh Ansh Ansh Ansh Ansh Ansh

Ansh Ansh Ansh Ansh

Ansh Ansh Ansh Ansh Ansh Ansh Ansh Ansh Ansh Ansh Ansh Ansh Ansh Ansh Ansh Ansh

Ansh Ansh Ansh Ansh Ansh Ansh Ansh Ansh Ansh Ansh Ansh Ansh Ansh Ansh Ansh Ansh

Ansh Ansh Ansh Ansh Ansh Ansh Ansh Ansh Ansh Ansh Ansh Ansh Ansh Ansh Ansh Ansh

Ansh Ansh Ansh Ansh Ansh Ansh Ansh Ansh Ansh Ansh Ansh Ansh Ansh Ansh Ansh Ansh

Ansh Ansh Ansh Ansh Ansh Ansh Ansh Ansh Ansh Ansh Ansh Ansh Ansh Ansh Ansh Ansh

Ansh Ansh Ansh Ansh Ansh Ansh Ansh Ansh Ansh Ansh Ansh Ansh Ansh Ansh Ansh Ansh

Ansh Ansh Ansh Ansh

Ansh Ansh Ansh Ansh Ansh Ansh Ansh Ansh Ansh Ansh Ansh Ansh Ansh Ansh Ansh Ansh

Ansh Ansh Ansh Ansh Ansh Ansh Ansh Ansh Ansh Ansh Ansh Ansh Ansh Ansh Ansh Ansh

Ansh Ansh Ansh Ansh Ansh Ansh Ansh Ansh Ansh Ansh Ansh Ansh Ansh Ansh Ansh Ansh

Ansh Ansh Ansh Ansh Ansh Ansh Ansh Ansh Ansh Ansh Ansh Ansh Ansh Ansh Ansh Ansh

Ansh Ansh Ansh Ansh Ansh Ansh Ansh Ansh Ansh Ansh Ansh Ansh Ansh Ansh Ansh Ansh

Ansh Ansh Ansh Ansh Ansh Ansh Ansh Ansh Ansh Ansh Ansh Ansh Ansh Ansh Ansh Ansh

Ansh Ansh Ansh Ansh

Ansh Ansh Ansh Ansh Ansh Ansh Ansh Ansh Ansh Ansh Ansh Ansh Ansh Ansh Ansh Ansh

Ansh Ansh Ansh Ansh Ansh Ansh Ansh Ansh Ansh Ansh Ansh Ansh Ansh Ansh Ansh Ansh

Ansh Ansh Ansh Ansh Ansh Ansh Ansh Ansh Ansh Ansh Ansh Ansh Ansh Ansh Ansh Ansh

Ansh Ansh Ansh Ansh Ansh Ansh Ansh Ansh Ansh Ansh Ansh Ansh Ansh Ansh Ansh Ansh

Ansh Ansh Ansh Ansh Ansh Ansh Ansh Ansh Ansh Ansh Ansh Ansh Ansh Ansh Ansh Ansh

Ansh Ansh Ansh Ansh Ansh Ansh Ansh Ansh Ansh Ansh Ansh Ansh Ansh Ansh Ansh Ansh

Ansh Ansh Ansh Ansh

Ansh Ansh Ansh Ansh Ansh Ansh Ansh Ansh Ansh Ansh Ansh Ansh Ansh Ansh Ansh Ansh

Ansh Ansh Ansh Ansh Ansh Ansh Ansh Ansh Ansh Ansh Ansh Ansh Ansh Ansh Ansh Ansh

Ansh Ansh Ansh Ansh Ansh Ansh Ansh Ansh Ansh Ansh Ansh Ansh Ansh Ansh Ansh Ansh

Ansh Ansh Ansh Ansh Ansh Ansh Ansh Ansh Ansh Ansh Ansh Ansh Ansh Ansh Ansh Ansh

Ansh Ansh Ansh Ansh Ansh Ansh Ansh Ansh Ansh Ansh Ansh Ansh Ansh Ansh Ansh Ansh

Ansh Ansh Ansh Ansh Ansh Ansh Ansh Ansh Ansh Ansh Ansh Ansh Ansh Ansh Ansh Ansh

Ansh Ansh Ansh Ansh

Ansh Ansh Ansh Ansh Ansh Ansh Ansh Ansh Ansh Ansh Ansh Ansh Ansh Ansh Ansh Ansh

Ansh Ansh Ansh Ansh Ansh Ansh Ansh Ansh Ansh Ansh Ansh Ansh Ansh Ansh Ansh Ansh

Ansh Ansh Ansh Ansh Ansh Ansh Ansh Ansh Ansh Ansh Ansh Ansh Ansh Ansh Ansh Ansh

Ansh Ansh Ansh Ansh Ansh Ansh Ansh Ansh Ansh Ansh Ansh Ansh Ansh Ansh Ansh Ansh

Ansh Ansh Ansh Ansh Ansh Ansh Ansh Ansh Ansh Ansh Ansh Ansh Ansh Ansh Ansh Ansh

Ansh Ansh Ansh Ansh Ansh Ansh Ansh Ansh Ansh Ansh Ansh Ansh Ansh Ansh Ansh Ansh

Ansh Ansh Ansh Ansh

Ansh Ansh Ansh Ansh Ansh Ansh Ansh Ansh Ansh Ansh Ansh Ansh Ansh Ansh Ansh Ansh

Ansh Ansh Ansh Ansh Ansh Ansh Ansh Ansh Ansh Ansh Ansh Ansh Ansh Ansh Ansh Ansh

Ansh Ansh Ansh Ansh Ansh Ansh Ansh Ansh Ansh Ansh Ansh Ansh Ansh Ansh Ansh Ansh

Ansh Ansh Ansh Ansh Ansh Ansh Ansh Ansh Ansh Ansh Ansh Ansh Ansh Ansh Ansh Ansh

Ansh Ansh Ansh Ansh Ansh Ansh Ansh Ansh Ansh Ansh Ansh Ansh Ansh Ansh Ansh Ansh

Ansh Ansh Ansh Ansh Ansh Ansh Ansh Ansh Ansh Ansh Ansh Ansh Ansh Ansh Ansh Ansh

Ansh Ansh Ansh Ansh

Ansh Ansh Ansh Ansh Ansh Ansh Ansh Ansh Ansh Ansh Ansh Ansh Ansh Ansh Ansh Ansh

Ansh Ansh Ansh Ansh Ansh Ansh Ansh Ansh Ansh Ansh Ansh Ansh Ansh Ansh Ansh Ansh

Ansh Ansh Ansh Ansh Ansh Ansh Ansh Ansh Ansh Ansh Ansh Ansh Ansh Ansh Ansh Ansh

Ansh Ansh Ansh Ansh Ansh Ansh Ansh Ansh Ansh Ansh Ansh Ansh Ansh Ansh Ansh Ansh

Ansh Ansh Ansh Ansh Ansh Ansh Ansh Ansh Ansh Ansh Ansh Ansh Ansh Ansh Ansh Ansh

Ansh Ansh Ansh Ansh Ansh Ansh Ansh Ansh Ansh Ansh Ansh Ansh Ansh Ansh Ansh Ansh

Ansh Ansh Ansh Ansh

Ansh Ansh Ansh Ansh Ansh Ansh Ansh Ansh Ansh Ansh Ansh Ansh

Ansh Ansh Ansh Ansh Ansh Ansh Ansh Ansh Ansh Ansh Ansh Ansh Ansh Ansh Ansh Ansh

Ansh Ansh Ansh Ansh Ansh Ansh Ansh Ansh Ansh Ansh Ansh Ansh Ansh Ansh Ansh Ansh

Ansh Ansh Ansh Ansh Ansh Ansh Ansh Ansh Ansh Ansh Ansh Ansh Ansh Ansh Ansh Ansh

Ansh Ansh Ansh Ansh Ansh Ansh Ansh Ansh Ansh Ansh Ansh Ansh Ansh Ansh Ansh Ansh

Ansh Ansh Ansh Ansh Ansh Ansh Ansh Ansh Ansh Ansh Ansh Ansh Ansh Ansh Ansh Ansh

Ansh Ansh Ansh Ansh

Ansh Ansh Ansh Ansh Ansh Ansh Ansh Ansh Ansh Ansh Ansh Ansh Ansh Ansh Ansh Ansh

Ansh Ansh Ansh Ansh Ansh Ansh Ansh Ansh Ansh Ansh Ansh Ansh Ansh Ansh Ansh Ansh

Ansh Ansh Ansh Ansh Ansh Ansh Ansh Ansh Ansh Ansh Ansh Ansh Ansh Ansh Ansh Ansh

Ansh Ansh Ansh Ansh Ansh Ansh Ansh Ansh Ansh Ansh Ansh Ansh Ansh Ansh Ansh Ansh

Ansh Ansh Ansh Ansh Ansh Ansh Ansh Ansh Ansh Ansh Ansh Ansh Ansh Ansh Ansh Ansh

Ansh Ansh Ansh Ansh Ansh Ansh Ansh Ansh Ansh Ansh Ansh Ansh Ansh Ansh Ansh Ansh

Ansh Ansh Ansh Ansh

Ansh Ansh Ansh Ansh Ansh Ansh Ansh Ansh Ansh Ansh Ansh Ansh Ansh Ansh Ansh Ansh

Ansh Ansh Ansh Ansh Ansh Ansh Ansh Ansh Ansh Ansh Ansh Ansh Ansh Ansh Ansh Ansh

Ansh Ansh Ansh Ansh Ansh Ansh Ansh Ansh Ansh Ansh Ansh Ansh Ansh Ansh Ansh Ansh

Ansh Ansh Ansh Ansh Ansh Ansh Ansh Ansh Ansh Ansh Ansh Ansh Ansh Ansh Ansh Ansh

Ansh Ansh Ansh Ansh Ansh Ansh Ansh Ansh Ansh Ansh Ansh Ansh Ansh Ansh Ansh Ansh

Ansh Ansh Ansh Ansh Ansh Ansh Ansh Ansh Ansh Ansh Ansh Ansh Ansh Ansh Ansh Ansh

Ansh Ansh Ansh Ansh

Ansh Ansh Ansh Ansh Ansh Ansh Ansh Ansh Ansh Ansh Ansh Ansh Ansh Ansh Ansh Ansh

Ansh Ansh Ansh Ansh Ansh Ansh Ansh Ansh Ansh Ansh Ansh Ansh Ansh Ansh Ansh Ansh

Ansh Ansh Ansh Ansh Ansh Ansh Ansh Ansh Ansh Ansh Ansh Ansh Ansh Ansh Ansh Ansh

Ansh Ansh Ansh Ansh Ansh Ansh Ansh Ansh Ansh Ansh Ansh Ansh Ansh Ansh Ansh Ansh

Ansh Ansh Ansh Ansh Ansh Ansh Ansh Ansh Ansh Ansh Ansh Ansh Ansh Ansh Ansh Ansh

Ansh Ansh Ansh Ansh Ansh Ansh Ansh Ansh Ansh Ansh Ansh Ansh Ansh Ansh Ansh Ansh

Ansh Ansh Ansh Ansh

Ansh Ansh Ansh Ansh Ansh Ansh Ansh Ansh Ansh Ansh Ansh Ansh Ansh Ansh Ansh Ansh

Ansh Ansh Ansh Ansh Ansh Ansh Ansh Ansh Ansh Ansh Ansh Ansh Ansh Ansh Ansh Ansh

Ansh Ansh Ansh Ansh Ansh Ansh Ansh Ansh Ansh Ansh Ansh Ansh Ansh Ansh Ansh Ansh

Ansh Ansh Ansh Ansh Ansh Ansh Ansh Ansh Ansh Ansh Ansh Ansh Ansh Ansh Ansh Ansh

Ansh Ansh Ansh Ansh Ansh Ansh Ansh Ansh Ansh Ansh Ansh Ansh Ansh Ansh Ansh Ansh

Ansh Ansh Ansh Ansh Ansh Ansh Ansh Ansh Ansh Ansh Ansh Ansh Ansh Ansh Ansh Ansh

Ansh Ansh Ansh Ansh

Ansh Ansh Ansh Ansh Ansh Ansh Ansh Ansh Ansh Ansh Ansh Ansh Ansh Ansh Ansh Ansh

Ansh Ansh Ansh Ansh Ansh Ansh Ansh Ansh Ansh Ansh Ansh Ansh Ansh Ansh Ansh Ansh

Ansh Ansh Ansh Ansh Ansh Ansh Ansh Ansh Ansh Ansh Ansh Ansh Ansh Ansh Ansh Ansh

Ansh Ansh Ansh Ansh Ansh Ansh Ansh Ansh Ansh Ansh Ansh Ansh Ansh Ansh Ansh Ansh

Ansh Ansh Ansh Ansh Ansh Ansh Ansh Ansh Ansh Ansh Ansh Ansh Ansh Ansh Ansh Ansh

Ansh Ansh Ansh Ansh Ansh Ansh Ansh Ansh Ansh Ansh Ansh Ansh Ansh Ansh Ansh Ansh

Ansh Ansh Ansh Ansh

Ansh Ansh Ansh Ansh Ansh Ansh Ansh Ansh Ansh Ansh Ansh Ansh Ansh Ansh Ansh Ansh

Ansh Ansh Ansh Ansh Ansh Ansh Ansh Ansh Ansh Ansh Ansh Ansh Ansh Ansh Ansh Ansh

Ansh Ansh Ansh Ansh Ansh Ansh Ansh Ansh Ansh Ansh Ansh Ansh Ansh Ansh Ansh Ansh

Ansh Ansh Ansh Ansh Ansh Ansh Ansh Ansh Ansh Ansh Ansh Ansh Ansh Ansh Ansh Ansh

Ansh Ansh Ansh Ansh Ansh Ansh Ansh Ansh Ansh Ansh Ansh Ansh Ansh Ansh Ansh Ansh

Ansh Ansh Ansh Ansh Ansh Ansh Ansh Ansh Ansh Ansh Ansh Ansh Ansh Ansh Ansh Ansh

Ansh Ansh Ansh Ansh

Ansh Ansh Ansh Ansh Ansh Ansh Ansh Ansh Ansh Ansh Ansh Ansh Ansh Ansh Ansh Ansh

Ansh Ansh Ansh Ansh Ansh Ansh Ansh Ansh Ansh Ansh Ansh Ansh Ansh Ansh Ansh Ansh

Ansh Ansh Ansh Ansh Ansh Ansh Ansh Ansh Ansh Ansh Ansh Ansh Ansh Ansh Ansh Ansh

Ansh Ansh Ansh Ansh Ansh Ansh Ansh Ansh Ansh Ansh Ansh Ansh Ansh Ansh Ansh Ansh

Ansh Ansh Ansh Ansh Ansh Ansh Ansh Ansh Ansh Ansh Ansh Ansh Ansh Ansh Ansh Ansh

Ansh Ansh Ansh Ansh Ansh Ansh Ansh Ansh Ansh Ansh Ansh Ansh Ansh Ansh Ansh Ansh

Ansh Ansh Ansh Ansh

Ansh Ansh Ansh Ansh Ansh Ansh Ansh Ansh Ansh Ansh Ansh Ansh Ansh Ansh Ansh Ansh

Ansh Ansh Ansh Ansh Ansh Ansh Ansh Ansh Ansh Ansh Ansh Ansh Ansh Ansh Ansh Ansh

Ansh Ansh Ansh Ansh Ansh Ansh Ansh Ansh Ansh Ansh Ansh Ansh Ansh Ansh Ansh Ansh

Ansh Ansh Ansh Ansh Ansh Ansh Ansh Ansh Ansh Ansh Ansh Ansh Ansh Ansh Ansh Ansh

Ansh Ansh Ansh Ansh Ansh Ansh Ansh Ansh Ansh Ansh Ansh Ansh Ansh Ansh Ansh Ansh

Ansh Ansh Ansh Ansh Ansh Ansh Ansh Ansh Ansh Ansh Ansh Ansh Ansh Ansh Ansh Ansh

Ansh Ansh Ansh Ansh

Ansh Ansh Ansh Ansh Ansh Ansh Ansh Ansh Ansh Ansh Ansh Ansh Ansh Ansh Ansh Ansh

Ansh Ansh Ansh Ansh Ansh Ansh Ansh Ansh Ansh Ansh Ansh Ansh Ansh Ansh Ansh Ansh

Ansh Ansh Ansh Ansh Ansh Ansh Ansh Ansh Ansh Ansh Ansh Ansh Ansh Ansh Ansh Ansh

Ansh Ansh Ansh Ansh Ansh Ansh Ansh Ansh Ansh Ansh Ansh Ansh Ansh Ansh Ansh Ansh

Ansh Ansh Ansh Ansh Ansh Ansh Ansh Ansh Ansh Ansh Ansh Ansh Ansh Ansh Ansh Ansh

Ansh Ansh Ansh Ansh Ansh Ansh Ansh Ansh Ansh Ansh Ansh Ansh Ansh Ansh Ansh Ansh

Ansh Ansh Ansh Ansh

Ansh Ansh Ansh Ansh Ansh Ansh Ansh Ansh Ansh Ansh Ansh Ansh

Ansh Ansh Ansh Ansh Ansh Ansh Ansh Ansh Ansh Ansh Ansh Ansh Ansh Ansh Ansh Ansh

Ansh Ansh Ansh Ansh Ansh Ansh Ansh Ansh Ansh Ansh Ansh Ansh Ansh Ansh Ansh Ansh

Ansh Ansh Ansh Ansh Ansh Ansh Ansh Ansh Ansh Ansh Ansh Ansh Ansh Ansh Ansh Ansh

Ansh Ansh Ansh Ansh Ansh Ansh Ansh Ansh Ansh Ansh Ansh Ansh Ansh Ansh Ansh Ansh

Ansh Ansh Ansh Ansh Ansh Ansh Ansh Ansh Ansh Ansh Ansh Ansh Ansh Ansh Ansh Ansh

Ansh Ansh Ansh Ansh

Ansh Ansh Ansh Ansh Ansh Ansh Ansh Ansh Ansh Ansh Ansh Ansh Ansh Ansh Ansh Ansh

Ansh Ansh Ansh Ansh Ansh Ansh Ansh Ansh Ansh Ansh Ansh Ansh Ansh Ansh Ansh Ansh

Ansh Ansh Ansh Ansh Ansh Ansh Ansh Ansh Ansh Ansh Ansh Ansh Ansh Ansh Ansh Ansh

Ansh Ansh Ansh Ansh Ansh Ansh Ansh Ansh Ansh Ansh Ansh Ansh Ansh Ansh Ansh Ansh

Ansh Ansh Ansh Ansh Ansh Ansh Ansh Ansh Ansh Ansh Ansh Ansh Ansh Ansh Ansh Ansh

Ansh Ansh Ansh Ansh Ansh Ansh Ansh Ansh Ansh Ansh Ansh Ansh Ansh Ansh Ansh Ansh

Ansh Ansh Ansh Ansh

Ansh Ansh Ansh Ansh Ansh Ansh Ansh Ansh Ansh Ansh Ansh Ansh Ansh Ansh Ansh Ansh

Ansh Ansh Ansh Ansh Ansh Ansh Ansh Ansh Ansh Ansh Ansh Ansh Ansh Ansh Ansh Ansh

Ansh Ansh Ansh Ansh Ansh Ansh Ansh Ansh Ansh Ansh Ansh Ansh Ansh Ansh Ansh Ansh

Ansh Ansh Ansh Ansh Ansh Ansh Ansh Ansh Ansh Ansh Ansh Ansh Ansh Ansh Ansh Ansh

Ansh Ansh Ansh Ansh Ansh Ansh Ansh Ansh Ansh Ansh Ansh Ansh Ansh Ansh Ansh Ansh

Ansh Ansh Ansh Ansh Ansh Ansh Ansh Ansh Ansh Ansh Ansh Ansh Ansh Ansh Ansh Ansh

Ansh Ansh Ansh Ansh

Ansh Ansh Ansh Ansh Ansh Ansh Ansh Ansh Ansh Ansh Ansh Ansh Ansh Ansh Ansh Ansh

Ansh Ansh Ansh Ansh Ansh Ansh Ansh Ansh Ansh Ansh Ansh Ansh Ansh Ansh Ansh Ansh

Ansh Ansh Ansh Ansh Ansh Ansh Ansh Ansh Ansh Ansh Ansh Ansh Ansh Ansh Ansh Ansh

Ansh Ansh Ansh Ansh Ansh Ansh Ansh Ansh Ansh Ansh Ansh Ansh Ansh Ansh Ansh Ansh

Ansh Ansh Ansh Ansh Ansh Ansh Ansh Ansh Ansh Ansh Ansh Ansh Ansh Ansh Ansh Ansh

Ansh Ansh Ansh Ansh Ansh Ansh Ansh Ansh Ansh Ansh Ansh Ansh Ansh Ansh Ansh Ansh

Ansh Ansh Ansh Ansh

Ansh Ansh Ansh Ansh Ansh Ansh Ansh Ansh Ansh Ansh Ansh Ansh Ansh Ansh Ansh Ansh

Ansh Ansh Ansh Ansh Ansh Ansh Ansh Ansh Ansh Ansh Ansh Ansh Ansh Ansh Ansh Ansh

Ansh Ansh Ansh Ansh Ansh Ansh Ansh Ansh Ansh Ansh Ansh Ansh Ansh Ansh Ansh Ansh

Ansh Ansh Ansh Ansh Ansh Ansh Ansh Ansh Ansh Ansh Ansh Ansh Ansh Ansh Ansh Ansh

Ansh Ansh Ansh Ansh Ansh Ansh Ansh Ansh Ansh Ansh Ansh Ansh Ansh Ansh Ansh Ansh

Ansh Ansh Ansh Ansh Ansh Ansh Ansh Ansh Ansh Ansh Ansh Ansh Ansh Ansh Ansh Ansh

Ansh Ansh Ansh Ansh

Ansh Ansh Ansh Ansh Ansh Ansh Ansh Ansh Ansh Ansh Ansh Ansh Ansh Ansh Ansh Ansh

Ansh Ansh Ansh Ansh Ansh Ansh Ansh Ansh Ansh Ansh Ansh Ansh Ansh Ansh Ansh Ansh

Ansh Ansh Ansh Ansh Ansh Ansh Ansh Ansh Ansh Ansh Ansh Ansh Ansh Ansh Ansh Ansh

Ansh Ansh Ansh Ansh Ansh Ansh Ansh Ansh Ansh Ansh Ansh Ansh Ansh Ansh Ansh Ansh

Ansh Ansh Ansh Ansh Ansh Ansh Ansh Ansh Ansh Ansh Ansh Ansh Ansh Ansh Ansh Ansh

Ansh Ansh Ansh Ansh Ansh Ansh Ansh Ansh Ansh Ansh Ansh Ansh Ansh Ansh Ansh Ansh

Ansh Ansh Ansh Ansh

Ansh Ansh Ansh Ansh Ansh Ansh Ansh Ansh Ansh Ansh Ansh Ansh Ansh Ansh Ansh Ansh

Ansh Ansh Ansh Ansh Ansh Ansh Ansh Ansh Ansh Ansh Ansh Ansh Ansh Ansh Ansh Ansh

Ansh Ansh Ansh Ansh Ansh Ansh Ansh Ansh Ansh Ansh Ansh Ansh Ansh Ansh Ansh Ansh

Ansh Ansh Ansh Ansh Ansh Ansh Ansh Ansh Ansh Ansh Ansh Ansh Ansh Ansh Ansh Ansh

Ansh Ansh Ansh Ansh Ansh Ansh Ansh Ansh Ansh Ansh Ansh Ansh Ansh Ansh Ansh Ansh

Ansh Ansh Ansh Ansh Ansh Ansh Ansh Ansh Ansh Ansh Ansh Ansh Ansh Ansh Ansh Ansh

Ansh Ansh Ansh Ansh

Ansh Ansh Ansh Ansh Ansh Ansh Ansh Ansh Ansh Ansh Ansh Ansh Ansh Ansh Ansh Ansh

Ansh Ansh Ansh Ansh Ansh Ansh Ansh Ansh Ansh Ansh Ansh Ansh Ansh Ansh Ansh Ansh

Ansh Ansh Ansh Ansh Ansh Ansh Ansh Ansh Ansh Ansh Ansh Ansh Ansh Ansh Ansh Ansh

Ansh Ansh Ansh Ansh Ansh Ansh Ansh Ansh Ansh Ansh Ansh Ansh Ansh Ansh Ansh Ansh

Ansh Ansh Ansh Ansh Ansh Ansh Ansh Ansh Ansh Ansh Ansh Ansh Ansh Ansh Ansh Ansh

Ansh Ansh Ansh Ansh Ansh Ansh Ansh Ansh Ansh Ansh Ansh Ansh Ansh Ansh Ansh Ansh

Ansh Ansh Ansh Ansh

Ansh Ansh Ansh Ansh Ansh Ansh Ansh Ansh Ansh Ansh Ansh Ansh Ansh Ansh Ansh Ansh

Ansh Ansh Ansh Ansh Ansh Ansh Ansh Ansh Ansh Ansh Ansh Ansh Ansh Ansh Ansh Ansh

Ansh Ansh Ansh Ansh Ansh Ansh Ansh Ansh Ansh Ansh Ansh Ansh Ansh Ansh Ansh Ansh

Ansh Ansh Ansh Ansh Ansh Ansh Ansh Ansh Ansh Ansh Ansh Ansh Ansh Ansh Ansh Ansh

Ansh Ansh Ansh Ansh Ansh Ansh Ansh Ansh Ansh Ansh Ansh Ansh Ansh Ansh Ansh Ansh

Ansh Ansh Ansh Ansh Ansh Ansh Ansh Ansh Ansh Ansh Ansh Ansh Ansh Ansh Ansh Ansh

Ansh Ansh Ansh Ansh

Ansh Ansh Ansh Ansh Ansh Ansh Ansh Ansh Ansh Ansh Ansh Ansh Ansh Ansh Ansh Ansh

Ansh Ansh Ansh Ansh Ansh Ansh Ansh Ansh Ansh Ansh Ansh Ansh Ansh Ansh Ansh Ansh

Ansh Ansh Ansh Ansh Ansh Ansh Ansh Ansh Ansh Ansh Ansh Ansh Ansh Ansh Ansh Ansh

Ansh Ansh Ansh Ansh Ansh Ansh Ansh Ansh Ansh Ansh Ansh Ansh Ansh Ansh Ansh Ansh

Ansh Ansh Ansh Ansh Ansh Ansh Ansh Ansh Ansh Ansh Ansh Ansh Ansh Ansh Ansh Ansh

Ansh Ansh Ansh Ansh Ansh Ansh Ansh Ansh Ansh Ansh Ansh Ansh Ansh Ansh Ansh Ansh

Ansh Ansh Ansh Ansh

Ansh Ansh Ansh Ansh Ansh Ansh Ansh Ansh Ansh Ansh Ansh Ansh

Ansh Ansh Ansh Ansh Ansh Ansh Ansh Ansh Ansh Ansh Ansh Ansh Ansh Ansh Ansh Ansh

Ansh Ansh Ansh Ansh Ansh Ansh Ansh Ansh Ansh Ansh Ansh Ansh Ansh Ansh Ansh Ansh

Ansh Ansh Ansh Ansh Ansh Ansh Ansh Ansh Ansh Ansh Ansh Ansh Ansh Ansh Ansh Ansh

Ansh Ansh Ansh Ansh Ansh Ansh Ansh Ansh Ansh Ansh Ansh Ansh Ansh Ansh Ansh Ansh

Ansh Ansh Ansh Ansh Ansh Ansh Ansh Ansh Ansh Ansh Ansh Ansh Ansh Ansh Ansh Ansh

Ansh Ansh Ansh Ansh

Ansh Ansh Ansh Ansh Ansh Ansh Ansh Ansh Ansh Ansh Ansh Ansh Ansh Ansh Ansh Ansh

Ansh Ansh Ansh Ansh Ansh Ansh Ansh Ansh Ansh Ansh Ansh Ansh Ansh Ansh Ansh Ansh

Ansh Ansh Ansh Ansh Ansh Ansh Ansh Ansh Ansh Ansh Ansh Ansh Ansh Ansh Ansh Ansh

Ansh Ansh Ansh Ansh Ansh Ansh Ansh Ansh Ansh Ansh Ansh Ansh Ansh Ansh Ansh Ansh

Ansh Ansh Ansh Ansh Ansh Ansh Ansh Ansh Ansh Ansh Ansh Ansh Ansh Ansh Ansh Ansh

Ansh Ansh Ansh Ansh Ansh Ansh Ansh Ansh Ansh Ansh Ansh Ansh Ansh Ansh Ansh Ansh

Ansh Ansh Ansh Ansh

Ansh Ansh Ansh Ansh Ansh Ansh Ansh Ansh Ansh Ansh Ansh Ansh Ansh Ansh Ansh Ansh

Ansh Ansh Ansh Ansh Ansh Ansh Ansh Ansh Ansh Ansh Ansh Ansh Ansh Ansh Ansh Ansh

Ansh Ansh Ansh Ansh Ansh Ansh Ansh Ansh Ansh Ansh Ansh Ansh Ansh Ansh Ansh Ansh

Ansh Ansh Ansh Ansh Ansh Ansh Ansh Ansh Ansh Ansh Ansh Ansh Ansh Ansh Ansh Ansh

Ansh Ansh Ansh Ansh Ansh Ansh Ansh Ansh Ansh Ansh Ansh Ansh Ansh Ansh Ansh Ansh

Ansh Ansh Ansh Ansh Ansh Ansh Ansh Ansh Ansh Ansh Ansh Ansh Ansh Ansh Ansh Ansh

Ansh Ansh Ansh Ansh

Ansh Ansh Ansh Ansh Ansh Ansh Ansh Ansh Ansh Ansh Ansh Ansh Ansh Ansh Ansh Ansh

Ansh Ansh Ansh Ansh Ansh Ansh Ansh Ansh Ansh Ansh Ansh Ansh Ansh Ansh Ansh Ansh

Ansh Ansh Ansh Ansh Ansh Ansh Ansh Ansh Ansh Ansh Ansh Ansh Ansh Ansh Ansh Ansh

Ansh Ansh Ansh Ansh Ansh Ansh Ansh Ansh Ansh Ansh Ansh Ansh Ansh Ansh Ansh Ansh

Ansh Ansh Ansh Ansh Ansh Ansh Ansh Ansh Ansh Ansh Ansh Ansh Ansh Ansh Ansh Ansh

Ansh Ansh Ansh Ansh Ansh Ansh Ansh Ansh Ansh Ansh Ansh Ansh Ansh Ansh Ansh Ansh

Ansh Ansh Ansh Ansh

Ansh Ansh Ansh Ansh Ansh Ansh Ansh Ansh Ansh Ansh Ansh Ansh Ansh Ansh Ansh Ansh

Ansh Ansh Ansh Ansh Ansh Ansh Ansh Ansh Ansh Ansh Ansh Ansh Ansh Ansh Ansh Ansh

Ansh Ansh Ansh Ansh Ansh Ansh Ansh Ansh Ansh Ansh Ansh Ansh Ansh Ansh Ansh Ansh

Ansh Ansh Ansh Ansh Ansh Ansh Ansh Ansh Ansh Ansh Ansh Ansh Ansh Ansh Ansh Ansh

Ansh Ansh Ansh Ansh Ansh Ansh Ansh Ansh Ansh Ansh Ansh Ansh Ansh Ansh Ansh Ansh

Ansh Ansh Ansh Ansh Ansh Ansh Ansh Ansh Ansh Ansh Ansh Ansh Ansh Ansh Ansh Ansh

Ansh Ansh Ansh Ansh

Ansh Ansh Ansh Ansh Ansh Ansh Ansh Ansh Ansh Ansh Ansh Ansh Ansh Ansh Ansh Ansh

Ansh Ansh Ansh Ansh Ansh Ansh Ansh Ansh Ansh Ansh Ansh Ansh Ansh Ansh Ansh Ansh

Ansh Ansh Ansh Ansh Ansh Ansh Ansh Ansh Ansh Ansh Ansh Ansh Ansh Ansh Ansh Ansh

Ansh Ansh Ansh Ansh Ansh Ansh Ansh Ansh Ansh Ansh Ansh Ansh Ansh Ansh Ansh Ansh

Ansh Ansh Ansh Ansh Ansh Ansh Ansh Ansh Ansh Ansh Ansh Ansh Ansh Ansh Ansh Ansh

Ansh Ansh Ansh Ansh Ansh Ansh Ansh Ansh Ansh Ansh Ansh Ansh Ansh Ansh Ansh Ansh

Ansh Ansh Ansh Ansh

Ansh Ansh Ansh Ansh Ansh Ansh Ansh Ansh Ansh Ansh Ansh Ansh Ansh Ansh Ansh Ansh

Ansh Ansh Ansh Ansh Ansh Ansh Ansh Ansh Ansh Ansh Ansh Ansh Ansh Ansh Ansh Ansh

Ansh Ansh Ansh Ansh Ansh Ansh Ansh Ansh Ansh Ansh Ansh Ansh Ansh Ansh Ansh Ansh

Ansh Ansh Ansh Ansh Ansh Ansh Ansh Ansh Ansh Ansh Ansh Ansh Ansh Ansh Ansh Ansh

Ansh Ansh Ansh Ansh Ansh Ansh Ansh Ansh Ansh Ansh Ansh Ansh Ansh Ansh Ansh Ansh

Ansh Ansh Ansh Ansh Ansh Ansh Ansh Ansh Ansh Ansh Ansh Ansh Ansh Ansh Ansh Ansh

Ansh Ansh Ansh Ansh

Ansh Ansh Ansh Ansh Ansh Ansh Ansh Ansh Ansh Ansh Ansh Ansh Ansh Ansh Ansh Ansh

Ansh Ansh Ansh Ansh Ansh Ansh Ansh Ansh Ansh Ansh Ansh Ansh Ansh Ansh Ansh Ansh

Ansh Ansh Ansh Ansh Ansh Ansh Ansh Ansh Ansh Ansh Ansh Ansh Ansh Ansh Ansh Ansh

Ansh Ansh Ansh Ansh Ansh Ansh Ansh Ansh Ansh Ansh Ansh Ansh Ansh Ansh Ansh Ansh

Ansh Ansh Ansh Ansh Ansh Ansh Ansh Ansh Ansh Ansh Ansh Ansh Ansh Ansh Ansh Ansh

Ansh Ansh Ansh Ansh Ansh Ansh Ansh Ansh Ansh Ansh Ansh Ansh Ansh Ansh Ansh Ansh

Ansh Ansh Ansh Ansh

Ansh Ansh Ansh Ansh Ansh Ansh Ansh Ansh Ansh Ansh Ansh Ansh Ansh Ansh Ansh Ansh

Ansh Ansh Ansh Ansh Ansh Ansh Ansh Ansh Ansh Ansh Ansh Ansh Ansh Ansh Ansh Ansh

Ansh Ansh Ansh Ansh Ansh Ansh Ansh Ansh Ansh Ansh Ansh Ansh Ansh Ansh Ansh Ansh

Ansh Ansh Ansh Ansh Ansh Ansh Ansh Ansh Ansh Ansh Ansh Ansh Ansh Ansh Ansh Ansh

Ansh Ansh Ansh Ansh Ansh Ansh Ansh Ansh Ansh Ansh Ansh Ansh Ansh Ansh Ansh Ansh

Ansh Ansh Ansh Ansh Ansh Ansh Ansh Ansh Ansh Ansh Ansh Ansh Ansh Ansh Ansh Ansh

Ansh Ansh Ansh Ansh

Ansh Ansh Ansh Ansh Ansh Ansh Ansh Ansh Ansh Ansh Ansh Ansh Ansh Ansh Ansh Ansh

Ansh Ansh Ansh Ansh Ansh Ansh Ansh Ansh Ansh Ansh Ansh Ansh Ansh Ansh Ansh Ansh

Ansh Ansh Ansh Ansh Ansh Ansh Ansh Ansh Ansh Ansh Ansh Ansh Ansh Ansh Ansh Ansh

Ansh Ansh Ansh Ansh Ansh Ansh Ansh Ansh Ansh Ansh Ansh Ansh Ansh Ansh Ansh Ansh

Ansh Ansh Ansh Ansh Ansh Ansh Ansh Ansh Ansh Ansh Ansh Ansh Ansh Ansh Ansh Ansh

Ansh Ansh Ansh Ansh Ansh Ansh Ansh Ansh Ansh Ansh Ansh Ansh Ansh Ansh Ansh Ansh

Ansh Ansh Ansh Ansh

Ansh Ansh Ansh Ansh Ansh Ansh Ansh Ansh Ansh Ansh Ansh Ansh

Ansh Ansh Ansh Ansh Ansh Ansh Ansh Ansh Ansh Ansh Ansh Ansh Ansh Ansh Ansh Ansh

Ansh Ansh Ansh Ansh Ansh Ansh Ansh Ansh Ansh Ansh Ansh Ansh Ansh Ansh Ansh Ansh

Ansh Ansh Ansh Ansh Ansh Ansh Ansh Ansh Ansh Ansh Ansh Ansh Ansh Ansh Ansh Ansh

Ansh Ansh Ansh Ansh Ansh Ansh Ansh Ansh Ansh Ansh Ansh Ansh Ansh Ansh Ansh Ansh

Ansh Ansh Ansh Ansh Ansh Ansh Ansh Ansh Ansh Ansh Ansh Ansh Ansh Ansh Ansh Ansh

Ansh Ansh Ansh Ansh

Ansh Ansh Ansh Ansh Ansh Ansh Ansh Ansh Ansh Ansh Ansh Ansh Ansh Ansh Ansh Ansh

Ansh Ansh Ansh Ansh Ansh Ansh Ansh Ansh Ansh Ansh Ansh Ansh Ansh Ansh Ansh Ansh

Ansh Ansh Ansh Ansh Ansh Ansh Ansh Ansh Ansh Ansh Ansh Ansh Ansh Ansh Ansh Ansh

Ansh Ansh Ansh Ansh Ansh Ansh Ansh Ansh Ansh Ansh Ansh Ansh Ansh Ansh Ansh Ansh

Ansh Ansh Ansh Ansh Ansh Ansh Ansh Ansh Ansh Ansh Ansh Ansh Ansh Ansh Ansh Ansh

Ansh Ansh Ansh Ansh Ansh Ansh Ansh Ansh Ansh Ansh Ansh Ansh Ansh Ansh Ansh Ansh

Ansh Ansh Ansh Ansh

Ansh Ansh Ansh Ansh Ansh Ansh Ansh Ansh Ansh Ansh Ansh Ansh Ansh Ansh Ansh Ansh

Ansh Ansh Ansh Ansh Ansh Ansh Ansh Ansh Ansh Ansh Ansh Ansh Ansh Ansh Ansh Ansh

Ansh Ansh Ansh Ansh Ansh Ansh Ansh Ansh Ansh Ansh Ansh Ansh Ansh Ansh Ansh Ansh

Ansh Ansh Ansh Ansh Ansh Ansh Ansh Ansh Ansh Ansh Ansh Ansh Ansh Ansh Ansh Ansh

Ansh Ansh Ansh Ansh Ansh Ansh Ansh Ansh Ansh Ansh Ansh Ansh Ansh Ansh Ansh Ansh

Ansh Ansh Ansh Ansh Ansh Ansh Ansh Ansh Ansh Ansh Ansh Ansh Ansh Ansh Ansh Ansh

Ansh Ansh Ansh Ansh

Ansh Ansh Ansh Ansh Ansh Ansh Ansh Ansh Ansh Ansh Ansh Ansh Ansh Ansh Ansh Ansh

Ansh Ansh Ansh Ansh Ansh Ansh Ansh Ansh Ansh Ansh Ansh Ansh Ansh Ansh Ansh Ansh

Ansh Ansh Ansh Ansh Ansh Ansh Ansh Ansh Ansh Ansh Ansh Ansh Ansh Ansh Ansh Ansh

Ansh Ansh Ansh Ansh Ansh Ansh Ansh Ansh Ansh Ansh Ansh Ansh Ansh Ansh Ansh Ansh

Ansh Ansh Ansh Ansh Ansh Ansh Ansh Ansh Ansh Ansh Ansh Ansh Ansh Ansh Ansh Ansh

Ansh Ansh Ansh Ansh Ansh Ansh Ansh Ansh Ansh Ansh Ansh Ansh Ansh Ansh Ansh Ansh

Ansh Ansh Ansh Ansh

Ansh Ansh Ansh Ansh Ansh Ansh Ansh Ansh Ansh Ansh Ansh Ansh Ansh Ansh Ansh Ansh

Ansh Ansh Ansh Ansh Ansh Ansh Ansh Ansh Ansh Ansh Ansh Ansh Ansh Ansh Ansh Ansh

Ansh Ansh Ansh Ansh Ansh Ansh Ansh Ansh Ansh Ansh Ansh Ansh Ansh Ansh Ansh Ansh

Ansh Ansh Ansh Ansh Ansh Ansh Ansh Ansh Ansh Ansh Ansh Ansh Ansh Ansh Ansh Ansh

Ansh Ansh Ansh Ansh Ansh Ansh Ansh Ansh Ansh Ansh Ansh Ansh Ansh Ansh Ansh Ansh

Ansh Ansh Ansh Ansh Ansh Ansh Ansh Ansh Ansh Ansh Ansh Ansh Ansh Ansh Ansh Ansh

Ansh Ansh Ansh Ansh

Ansh Ansh Ansh Ansh Ansh Ansh Ansh Ansh Ansh Ansh Ansh Ansh Ansh Ansh Ansh Ansh

Ansh Ansh Ansh Ansh Ansh Ansh Ansh Ansh Ansh Ansh Ansh Ansh Ansh Ansh Ansh Ansh

Ansh Ansh Ansh Ansh Ansh Ansh Ansh Ansh Ansh Ansh Ansh Ansh Ansh Ansh Ansh Ansh

Ansh Ansh Ansh Ansh Ansh Ansh Ansh Ansh Ansh Ansh Ansh Ansh Ansh Ansh Ansh Ansh

Ansh Ansh Ansh Ansh Ansh Ansh Ansh Ansh Ansh Ansh Ansh Ansh Ansh Ansh Ansh Ansh

Ansh Ansh Ansh Ansh Ansh Ansh Ansh Ansh Ansh Ansh Ansh Ansh Ansh Ansh Ansh Ansh

Ansh Ansh Ansh Ansh

Ansh Ansh Ansh Ansh Ansh Ansh Ansh Ansh Ansh Ansh Ansh Ansh Ansh Ansh Ansh Ansh

Ansh Ansh Ansh Ansh Ansh Ansh Ansh Ansh Ansh Ansh Ansh Ansh Ansh Ansh Ansh Ansh

Ansh Ansh Ansh Ansh Ansh Ansh Ansh Ansh Ansh Ansh Ansh Ansh Ansh Ansh Ansh Ansh

Ansh Ansh Ansh Ansh Ansh Ansh Ansh Ansh Ansh Ansh Ansh Ansh Ansh Ansh Ansh Ansh

Ansh Ansh Ansh Ansh Ansh Ansh Ansh Ansh Ansh Ansh Ansh Ansh Ansh Ansh Ansh Ansh

Ansh Ansh Ansh Ansh Ansh Ansh Ansh Ansh Ansh Ansh Ansh Ansh Ansh Ansh Ansh Ansh

Ansh Ansh Ansh Ansh

Ansh Ansh Ansh Ansh Ansh Ansh Ansh Ansh Ansh Ansh Ansh Ansh Ansh Ansh Ansh Ansh

Ansh Ansh Ansh Ansh Ansh Ansh Ansh Ansh Ansh Ansh Ansh Ansh Ansh Ansh Ansh Ansh

Ansh Ansh Ansh Ansh Ansh Ansh Ansh Ansh Ansh Ansh Ansh Ansh Ansh Ansh Ansh Ansh

Ansh Ansh Ansh Ansh Ansh Ansh Ansh Ansh Ansh Ansh Ansh Ansh Ansh Ansh Ansh Ansh

Ansh Ansh Ansh Ansh Ansh Ansh Ansh Ansh Ansh Ansh Ansh Ansh Ansh Ansh Ansh Ansh

Ansh Ansh Ansh Ansh Ansh Ansh Ansh Ansh Ansh Ansh Ansh Ansh Ansh Ansh Ansh Ansh

Ansh Ansh Ansh Ansh

Ansh Ansh Ansh Ansh Ansh Ansh Ansh Ansh Ansh Ansh Ansh Ansh Ansh Ansh Ansh Ansh

Ansh Ansh Ansh Ansh Ansh Ansh Ansh Ansh Ansh Ansh Ansh Ansh Ansh Ansh Ansh Ansh

Ansh Ansh Ansh Ansh Ansh Ansh Ansh Ansh Ansh Ansh Ansh Ansh Ansh Ansh Ansh Ansh

Ansh Ansh Ansh Ansh Ansh Ansh Ansh Ansh Ansh Ansh Ansh Ansh Ansh Ansh Ansh Ansh

Ansh Ansh Ansh Ansh Ansh Ansh Ansh Ansh Ansh Ansh Ansh Ansh Ansh Ansh Ansh Ansh

Ansh Ansh Ansh Ansh Ansh Ansh Ansh Ansh Ansh Ansh Ansh Ansh Ansh Ansh Ansh Ansh

Ansh Ansh Ansh Ansh

Ansh Ansh Ansh Ansh Ansh Ansh Ansh Ansh Ansh Ansh Ansh Ansh Ansh Ansh Ansh Ansh

Ansh Ansh Ansh Ansh Ansh Ansh Ansh Ansh Ansh Ansh Ansh Ansh Ansh Ansh Ansh Ansh

Ansh Ansh Ansh Ansh Ansh Ansh Ansh Ansh Ansh Ansh Ansh Ansh Ansh Ansh Ansh Ansh

Ansh Ansh Ansh Ansh Ansh Ansh Ansh Ansh Ansh Ansh Ansh Ansh Ansh Ansh Ansh Ansh

Ansh Ansh Ansh Ansh Ansh Ansh Ansh Ansh Ansh Ansh Ansh Ansh Ansh Ansh Ansh Ansh

Ansh Ansh Ansh Ansh Ansh Ansh Ansh Ansh Ansh Ansh Ansh Ansh Ansh Ansh Ansh Ansh

Ansh Ansh Ansh Ansh

Ansh Ansh Ansh Ansh Ansh Ansh Ansh Ansh Ansh Ansh Ansh Ansh

Ansh Ansh Ansh Ansh Ansh Ansh Ansh Ansh Ansh Ansh Ansh Ansh Ansh Ansh Ansh Ansh

Ansh Ansh Ansh Ansh Ansh Ansh Ansh Ansh Ansh Ansh Ansh Ansh Ansh Ansh Ansh Ansh

Ansh Ansh Ansh Ansh Ansh Ansh Ansh Ansh Ansh Ansh Ansh Ansh Ansh Ansh Ansh Ansh

Ansh Ansh Ansh Ansh Ansh Ansh Ansh Ansh Ansh Ansh Ansh Ansh Ansh Ansh Ansh Ansh

Ansh Ansh Ansh Ansh Ansh Ansh Ansh Ansh Ansh Ansh Ansh Ansh Ansh Ansh Ansh Ansh

Ansh Ansh Ansh Ansh

Ansh Ansh Ansh Ansh Ansh Ansh Ansh Ansh Ansh Ansh Ansh Ansh Ansh Ansh Ansh Ansh

Ansh Ansh Ansh Ansh Ansh Ansh Ansh Ansh Ansh Ansh Ansh Ansh Ansh Ansh Ansh Ansh

Ansh Ansh Ansh Ansh Ansh Ansh Ansh Ansh Ansh Ansh Ansh Ansh Ansh Ansh Ansh Ansh

Ansh Ansh Ansh Ansh Ansh Ansh Ansh Ansh Ansh Ansh Ansh Ansh Ansh Ansh Ansh Ansh

Ansh Ansh Ansh Ansh Ansh Ansh Ansh Ansh Ansh Ansh Ansh Ansh Ansh Ansh Ansh Ansh

Ansh Ansh Ansh Ansh Ansh Ansh Ansh Ansh Ansh Ansh Ansh Ansh Ansh Ansh Ansh Ansh

Ansh Ansh Ansh Ansh

Ansh Ansh Ansh Ansh Ansh Ansh Ansh Ansh Ansh Ansh Ansh Ansh Ansh Ansh Ansh Ansh

Ansh Ansh Ansh Ansh Ansh Ansh Ansh Ansh Ansh Ansh Ansh Ansh Ansh Ansh Ansh Ansh

Ansh Ansh Ansh Ansh Ansh Ansh Ansh Ansh Ansh Ansh Ansh Ansh Ansh Ansh Ansh Ansh

Ansh Ansh Ansh Ansh Ansh Ansh Ansh Ansh Ansh Ansh Ansh Ansh Ansh Ansh Ansh Ansh

Ansh Ansh Ansh Ansh Ansh Ansh Ansh Ansh Ansh Ansh Ansh Ansh Ansh Ansh Ansh Ansh

Ansh Ansh Ansh Ansh Ansh Ansh Ansh Ansh Ansh Ansh Ansh Ansh Ansh Ansh Ansh Ansh

Ansh Ansh Ansh Ansh

Ansh Ansh Ansh Ansh Ansh Ansh Ansh Ansh Ansh Ansh Ansh Ansh Ansh Ansh Ansh Ansh

Ansh Ansh Ansh Ansh Ansh Ansh Ansh Ansh Ansh Ansh Ansh Ansh Ansh Ansh Ansh Ansh

Ansh Ansh Ansh Ansh Ansh Ansh Ansh Ansh Ansh Ansh Ansh Ansh Ansh Ansh Ansh Ansh

Ansh Ansh Ansh Ansh Ansh Ansh Ansh Ansh Ansh Ansh Ansh Ansh Ansh Ansh Ansh Ansh

Ansh Ansh Ansh Ansh Ansh Ansh Ansh Ansh Ansh Ansh Ansh Ansh Ansh Ansh Ansh Ansh

Ansh Ansh Ansh Ansh Ansh Ansh Ansh Ansh Ansh Ansh Ansh Ansh Ansh Ansh Ansh Ansh

Ansh Ansh Ansh Ansh

Ansh Ansh Ansh Ansh Ansh Ansh Ansh Ansh Ansh Ansh Ansh Ansh Ansh Ansh Ansh Ansh

Ansh Ansh Ansh Ansh Ansh Ansh Ansh Ansh Ansh Ansh Ansh Ansh Ansh Ansh Ansh Ansh

Ansh Ansh Ansh Ansh Ansh Ansh Ansh Ansh Ansh Ansh Ansh Ansh Ansh Ansh Ansh Ansh

Ansh Ansh Ansh Ansh Ansh Ansh Ansh Ansh Ansh Ansh Ansh Ansh Ansh Ansh Ansh Ansh

Ansh Ansh Ansh Ansh Ansh Ansh Ansh Ansh Ansh Ansh Ansh Ansh Ansh Ansh Ansh Ansh

Ansh Ansh Ansh Ansh Ansh Ansh Ansh Ansh Ansh Ansh Ansh Ansh Ansh Ansh Ansh Ansh

Ansh Ansh Ansh Ansh

Ansh Ansh Ansh Ansh Ansh Ansh Ansh Ansh Ansh Ansh Ansh Ansh Ansh Ansh Ansh Ansh

Ansh Ansh Ansh Ansh Ansh Ansh Ansh Ansh Ansh Ansh Ansh Ansh Ansh Ansh Ansh Ansh

Ansh Ansh Ansh Ansh Ansh Ansh Ansh Ansh Ansh Ansh Ansh Ansh Ansh Ansh Ansh Ansh

Ansh Ansh Ansh Ansh Ansh Ansh Ansh Ansh Ansh Ansh Ansh Ansh Ansh Ansh Ansh Ansh

Ansh Ansh Ansh Ansh Ansh Ansh Ansh Ansh Ansh Ansh Ansh Ansh Ansh Ansh Ansh Ansh

Ansh Ansh Ansh Ansh Ansh Ansh Ansh Ansh Ansh Ansh Ansh Ansh Ansh Ansh Ansh Ansh

Ansh Ansh Ansh Ansh

Ansh Ansh Ansh Ansh Ansh Ansh Ansh Ansh Ansh Ansh Ansh Ansh Ansh Ansh Ansh Ansh

Ansh Ansh Ansh Ansh Ansh Ansh Ansh Ansh Ansh Ansh Ansh Ansh Ansh Ansh Ansh Ansh

Ansh Ansh Ansh Ansh Ansh Ansh Ansh Ansh Ansh Ansh Ansh Ansh Ansh Ansh Ansh Ansh

Ansh Ansh Ansh Ansh Ansh Ansh Ansh Ansh Ansh Ansh Ansh Ansh Ansh Ansh Ansh Ansh

Ansh Ansh Ansh Ansh Ansh Ansh Ansh Ansh Ansh Ansh Ansh Ansh Ansh Ansh Ansh Ansh

Ansh Ansh Ansh Ansh Ansh Ansh Ansh Ansh Ansh Ansh Ansh Ansh Ansh Ansh Ansh Ansh

Ansh Ansh Ansh Ansh

Ansh Ansh Ansh Ansh Ansh Ansh Ansh Ansh Ansh Ansh Ansh Ansh Ansh Ansh Ansh Ansh

Ansh Ansh Ansh Ansh Ansh Ansh Ansh Ansh Ansh Ansh Ansh Ansh Ansh Ansh Ansh Ansh

Ansh Ansh Ansh Ansh Ansh Ansh Ansh Ansh Ansh Ansh Ansh Ansh Ansh Ansh Ansh Ansh

Ansh Ansh Ansh Ansh Ansh Ansh Ansh Ansh Ansh Ansh Ansh Ansh Ansh Ansh Ansh Ansh

Ansh Ansh Ansh Ansh Ansh Ansh Ansh Ansh Ansh Ansh Ansh Ansh Ansh Ansh Ansh Ansh

Ansh Ansh Ansh Ansh Ansh Ansh Ansh Ansh Ansh Ansh Ansh Ansh Ansh Ansh Ansh Ansh

Ansh Ansh Ansh Ansh

Ansh Ansh Ansh Ansh Ansh Ansh Ansh Ansh Ansh Ansh Ansh Ansh Ansh Ansh Ansh Ansh

Ansh Ansh Ansh Ansh Ansh Ansh Ansh Ansh Ansh Ansh Ansh Ansh Ansh Ansh Ansh Ansh

Ansh Ansh Ansh Ansh Ansh Ansh Ansh Ansh Ansh Ansh Ansh Ansh Ansh Ansh Ansh Ansh

Ansh Ansh Ansh Ansh Ansh Ansh Ansh Ansh Ansh Ansh Ansh Ansh Ansh Ansh Ansh Ansh

Ansh Ansh Ansh Ansh Ansh Ansh Ansh Ansh Ansh Ansh Ansh Ansh Ansh Ansh Ansh Ansh

Ansh Ansh Ansh Ansh Ansh Ansh Ansh Ansh Ansh Ansh Ansh Ansh Ansh Ansh Ansh Ansh

Ansh Ansh Ansh Ansh

Ansh Ansh Ansh Ansh Ansh Ansh Ansh Ansh Ansh Ansh Ansh Ansh Ansh Ansh Ansh Ansh

Ansh Ansh Ansh Ansh Ansh Ansh Ansh Ansh Ansh Ansh Ansh Ansh Ansh Ansh Ansh Ansh

Ansh Ansh Ansh Ansh Ansh Ansh Ansh Ansh Ansh Ansh Ansh Ansh Ansh Ansh Ansh Ansh

Ansh Ansh Ansh Ansh Ansh Ansh Ansh Ansh Ansh Ansh Ansh Ansh Ansh Ansh Ansh Ansh

Ansh Ansh Ansh Ansh Ansh Ansh Ansh Ansh Ansh Ansh Ansh Ansh Ansh Ansh Ansh Ansh

Ansh Ansh Ansh Ansh Ansh Ansh Ansh Ansh Ansh Ansh Ansh Ansh Ansh Ansh Ansh Ansh

Ansh Ansh Ansh Ansh

Ansh Ansh Ansh Ansh Ansh Ansh Ansh Ansh Ansh Ansh Ansh Ansh

Ansh Ansh Ansh Ansh Ansh Ansh Ansh Ansh Ansh Ansh Ansh Ansh Ansh Ansh Ansh Ansh

Ansh Ansh Ansh Ansh Ansh Ansh Ansh Ansh Ansh Ansh Ansh Ansh Ansh Ansh Ansh Ansh

Ansh Ansh Ansh Ansh Ansh Ansh Ansh Ansh Ansh Ansh Ansh Ansh Ansh Ansh Ansh Ansh

Ansh Ansh Ansh Ansh Ansh Ansh Ansh Ansh Ansh Ansh Ansh Ansh Ansh Ansh Ansh Ansh

Ansh Ansh Ansh Ansh Ansh Ansh Ansh Ansh Ansh Ansh Ansh Ansh Ansh Ansh Ansh Ansh

Ansh Ansh Ansh Ansh

Ansh Ansh Ansh Ansh Ansh Ansh Ansh Ansh Ansh Ansh Ansh Ansh Ansh Ansh Ansh Ansh

Ansh Ansh Ansh Ansh Ansh Ansh Ansh Ansh Ansh Ansh Ansh Ansh Ansh Ansh Ansh Ansh

Ansh Ansh Ansh Ansh Ansh Ansh Ansh Ansh Ansh Ansh Ansh Ansh Ansh Ansh Ansh Ansh

Ansh Ansh Ansh Ansh Ansh Ansh Ansh Ansh Ansh Ansh Ansh Ansh Ansh Ansh Ansh Ansh

Ansh Ansh Ansh Ansh Ansh Ansh Ansh Ansh Ansh Ansh Ansh Ansh Ansh Ansh Ansh Ansh

Ansh Ansh Ansh Ansh Ansh Ansh Ansh Ansh Ansh Ansh Ansh Ansh Ansh Ansh Ansh Ansh

Ansh Ansh Ansh Ansh

Ansh Ansh Ansh Ansh Ansh Ansh Ansh Ansh Ansh Ansh Ansh Ansh Ansh Ansh Ansh Ansh

Ansh Ansh Ansh Ansh Ansh Ansh Ansh Ansh Ansh Ansh Ansh Ansh Ansh Ansh Ansh Ansh

Ansh Ansh Ansh Ansh Ansh Ansh Ansh Ansh Ansh Ansh Ansh Ansh Ansh Ansh Ansh Ansh

Ansh Ansh Ansh Ansh Ansh Ansh Ansh Ansh Ansh Ansh Ansh Ansh Ansh Ansh Ansh Ansh

Ansh Ansh Ansh Ansh Ansh Ansh Ansh Ansh Ansh Ansh Ansh Ansh Ansh Ansh Ansh Ansh

Ansh Ansh Ansh Ansh Ansh Ansh Ansh Ansh Ansh Ansh Ansh Ansh Ansh Ansh Ansh Ansh

Ansh Ansh Ansh Ansh

Ansh Ansh Ansh Ansh Ansh Ansh Ansh Ansh Ansh Ansh Ansh Ansh Ansh Ansh Ansh Ansh

Ansh Ansh Ansh Ansh Ansh Ansh Ansh Ansh Ansh Ansh Ansh Ansh Ansh Ansh Ansh Ansh

Ansh Ansh Ansh Ansh Ansh Ansh Ansh Ansh Ansh Ansh Ansh Ansh Ansh Ansh Ansh Ansh

Ansh Ansh Ansh Ansh Ansh Ansh Ansh Ansh Ansh Ansh Ansh Ansh Ansh Ansh Ansh Ansh

Ansh Ansh Ansh Ansh Ansh Ansh Ansh Ansh Ansh Ansh Ansh Ansh Ansh Ansh Ansh Ansh

Ansh Ansh Ansh Ansh Ansh Ansh Ansh Ansh Ansh Ansh Ansh Ansh Ansh Ansh Ansh Ansh

Ansh Ansh Ansh Ansh

Ansh Ansh Ansh Ansh Ansh Ansh Ansh Ansh Ansh Ansh Ansh Ansh Ansh Ansh Ansh Ansh

Ansh Ansh Ansh Ansh Ansh Ansh Ansh Ansh Ansh Ansh Ansh Ansh Ansh Ansh Ansh Ansh

Ansh Ansh Ansh Ansh Ansh Ansh Ansh Ansh Ansh Ansh Ansh Ansh Ansh Ansh Ansh Ansh

Ansh Ansh Ansh Ansh Ansh Ansh Ansh Ansh Ansh Ansh Ansh Ansh Ansh Ansh Ansh Ansh

Ansh Ansh Ansh Ansh Ansh Ansh Ansh Ansh Ansh Ansh Ansh Ansh Ansh Ansh Ansh Ansh

Ansh Ansh Ansh Ansh Ansh Ansh Ansh Ansh Ansh Ansh Ansh Ansh Ansh Ansh Ansh Ansh

Ansh Ansh Ansh Ansh

Ansh Ansh Ansh Ansh Ansh Ansh Ansh Ansh Ansh Ansh Ansh Ansh Ansh Ansh Ansh Ansh

Ansh Ansh Ansh Ansh Ansh Ansh Ansh Ansh Ansh Ansh Ansh Ansh Ansh Ansh Ansh Ansh

Ansh Ansh Ansh Ansh Ansh Ansh Ansh Ansh Ansh Ansh Ansh Ansh Ansh Ansh Ansh Ansh

Ansh Ansh Ansh Ansh Ansh Ansh Ansh Ansh Ansh Ansh Ansh Ansh Ansh Ansh Ansh Ansh

Ansh Ansh Ansh Ansh Ansh Ansh Ansh Ansh Ansh Ansh Ansh Ansh Ansh Ansh Ansh Ansh

Ansh Ansh Ansh Ansh Ansh Ansh Ansh Ansh Ansh Ansh Ansh Ansh Ansh Ansh Ansh Ansh

Ansh Ansh Ansh Ansh

Ansh Ansh Ansh Ansh Ansh Ansh Ansh Ansh Ansh Ansh Ansh Ansh Ansh Ansh Ansh Ansh

Ansh Ansh Ansh Ansh Ansh Ansh Ansh Ansh Ansh Ansh Ansh Ansh Ansh Ansh Ansh Ansh

Ansh Ansh Ansh Ansh Ansh Ansh Ansh Ansh Ansh Ansh Ansh Ansh Ansh Ansh Ansh Ansh

Ansh Ansh Ansh Ansh Ansh Ansh Ansh Ansh Ansh Ansh Ansh Ansh Ansh Ansh Ansh Ansh

Ansh Ansh Ansh Ansh Ansh Ansh Ansh Ansh Ansh Ansh Ansh Ansh Ansh Ansh Ansh Ansh

Ansh Ansh Ansh Ansh Ansh Ansh Ansh Ansh Ansh Ansh Ansh Ansh Ansh Ansh Ansh Ansh

Ansh Ansh Ansh Ansh

Ansh Ansh Ansh Ansh Ansh Ansh Ansh Ansh Ansh Ansh Ansh Ansh Ansh Ansh Ansh Ansh

Ansh Ansh Ansh Ansh Ansh Ansh Ansh Ansh Ansh Ansh Ansh Ansh Ansh Ansh Ansh Ansh

Ansh Ansh Ansh Ansh Ansh Ansh Ansh Ansh Ansh Ansh Ansh Ansh Ansh Ansh Ansh Ansh

Ansh Ansh Ansh Ansh Ansh Ansh Ansh Ansh Ansh Ansh Ansh Ansh Ansh Ansh Ansh Ansh

Ansh Ansh Ansh Ansh Ansh Ansh Ansh Ansh Ansh Ansh Ansh Ansh Ansh Ansh Ansh Ansh

Ansh Ansh Ansh Ansh Ansh Ansh Ansh Ansh Ansh Ansh Ansh Ansh Ansh Ansh Ansh Ansh

Ansh Ansh Ansh Ansh

Ansh Ansh Ansh Ansh Ansh Ansh Ansh Ansh Ansh Ansh Ansh Ansh Ansh Ansh Ansh Ansh

Ansh Ansh Ansh Ansh Ansh Ansh Ansh Ansh Ansh Ansh Ansh Ansh Ansh Ansh Ansh Ansh

Ansh Ansh Ansh Ansh Ansh Ansh Ansh Ansh Ansh Ansh Ansh Ansh Ansh Ansh Ansh Ansh

Ansh Ansh Ansh Ansh Ansh Ansh Ansh Ansh Ansh Ansh Ansh Ansh Ansh Ansh Ansh Ansh

Ansh Ansh Ansh Ansh Ansh Ansh Ansh Ansh Ansh Ansh Ansh Ansh Ansh Ansh Ansh Ansh

Ansh Ansh Ansh Ansh Ansh Ansh Ansh Ansh Ansh Ansh Ansh Ansh Ansh Ansh Ansh Ansh

Ansh Ansh Ansh Ansh

Ansh Ansh Ansh Ansh Ansh Ansh Ansh Ansh Ansh Ansh Ansh Ansh Ansh Ansh Ansh Ansh

Ansh Ansh Ansh Ansh Ansh Ansh Ansh Ansh Ansh Ansh Ansh Ansh Ansh Ansh Ansh Ansh

Ansh Ansh Ansh Ansh Ansh Ansh Ansh Ansh Ansh Ansh Ansh Ansh Ansh Ansh Ansh Ansh

Ansh Ansh Ansh Ansh Ansh Ansh Ansh Ansh Ansh Ansh Ansh Ansh Ansh Ansh Ansh Ansh

Ansh Ansh Ansh Ansh Ansh Ansh Ansh Ansh Ansh Ansh Ansh Ansh Ansh Ansh Ansh Ansh

Ansh Ansh Ansh Ansh Ansh Ansh Ansh Ansh Ansh Ansh Ansh Ansh Ansh Ansh Ansh Ansh

Ansh Ansh Ansh Ansh

Ansh Ansh Ansh Ansh Ansh Ansh Ansh Ansh Ansh Ansh Ansh Ansh

Ansh Ansh Ansh Ansh Ansh Ansh Ansh Ansh Ansh Ansh Ansh Ansh Ansh Ansh Ansh Ansh

Ansh Ansh Ansh Ansh Ansh Ansh Ansh Ansh Ansh Ansh Ansh Ansh Ansh Ansh Ansh Ansh

Ansh Ansh Ansh Ansh Ansh Ansh Ansh Ansh Ansh Ansh Ansh Ansh Ansh Ansh Ansh Ansh

Ansh Ansh Ansh Ansh Ansh Ansh Ansh Ansh Ansh Ansh Ansh Ansh Ansh Ansh Ansh Ansh

Ansh Ansh Ansh Ansh Ansh Ansh Ansh Ansh Ansh Ansh Ansh Ansh Ansh Ansh Ansh Ansh

Ansh Ansh Ansh Ansh

Ansh Ansh Ansh Ansh Ansh Ansh Ansh Ansh Ansh Ansh Ansh Ansh Ansh Ansh Ansh Ansh

Ansh Ansh Ansh Ansh Ansh Ansh Ansh Ansh Ansh Ansh Ansh Ansh Ansh Ansh Ansh Ansh

Ansh Ansh Ansh Ansh Ansh Ansh Ansh Ansh Ansh Ansh Ansh Ansh Ansh Ansh Ansh Ansh

Ansh Ansh Ansh Ansh Ansh Ansh Ansh Ansh Ansh Ansh Ansh Ansh Ansh Ansh Ansh Ansh

Ansh Ansh Ansh Ansh Ansh Ansh Ansh Ansh Ansh Ansh Ansh Ansh Ansh Ansh Ansh Ansh

Ansh Ansh Ansh Ansh Ansh Ansh Ansh Ansh Ansh Ansh Ansh Ansh Ansh Ansh Ansh Ansh

Ansh Ansh Ansh Ansh

Ansh Ansh Ansh Ansh Ansh Ansh Ansh Ansh Ansh Ansh Ansh Ansh Ansh Ansh Ansh Ansh

Ansh Ansh Ansh Ansh Ansh Ansh Ansh Ansh Ansh Ansh Ansh Ansh Ansh Ansh Ansh Ansh

Ansh Ansh Ansh Ansh Ansh Ansh Ansh Ansh Ansh Ansh Ansh Ansh Ansh Ansh Ansh Ansh

Ansh Ansh Ansh Ansh Ansh Ansh Ansh Ansh Ansh Ansh Ansh Ansh Ansh Ansh Ansh Ansh

Ansh Ansh Ansh Ansh Ansh Ansh Ansh Ansh Ansh Ansh Ansh Ansh Ansh Ansh Ansh Ansh

Ansh Ansh Ansh Ansh Ansh Ansh Ansh Ansh Ansh Ansh Ansh Ansh Ansh Ansh Ansh Ansh

Ansh Ansh Ansh Ansh

Ansh Ansh Ansh Ansh Ansh Ansh Ansh Ansh Ansh Ansh Ansh Ansh Ansh Ansh Ansh Ansh

Ansh Ansh Ansh Ansh Ansh Ansh Ansh Ansh Ansh Ansh Ansh Ansh Ansh Ansh Ansh Ansh

Ansh Ansh Ansh Ansh Ansh Ansh Ansh Ansh Ansh Ansh Ansh Ansh Ansh Ansh Ansh Ansh

Ansh Ansh Ansh Ansh Ansh Ansh Ansh Ansh Ansh Ansh Ansh Ansh Ansh Ansh Ansh Ansh

Ansh Ansh Ansh Ansh Ansh Ansh Ansh Ansh Ansh Ansh Ansh Ansh Ansh Ansh Ansh Ansh

Ansh Ansh Ansh Ansh Ansh Ansh Ansh Ansh Ansh Ansh Ansh Ansh Ansh Ansh Ansh Ansh

Ansh Ansh Ansh Ansh

Ansh Ansh Ansh Ansh Ansh Ansh Ansh Ansh Ansh Ansh Ansh Ansh Ansh Ansh Ansh Ansh

Ansh Ansh Ansh Ansh Ansh Ansh Ansh Ansh Ansh Ansh Ansh Ansh Ansh Ansh Ansh Ansh

Ansh Ansh Ansh Ansh Ansh Ansh Ansh Ansh Ansh Ansh Ansh Ansh Ansh Ansh Ansh Ansh

Ansh Ansh Ansh Ansh Ansh Ansh Ansh Ansh Ansh Ansh Ansh Ansh Ansh Ansh Ansh Ansh

Ansh Ansh Ansh Ansh Ansh Ansh Ansh Ansh Ansh Ansh Ansh Ansh Ansh Ansh Ansh Ansh

Ansh Ansh Ansh Ansh Ansh Ansh Ansh Ansh Ansh Ansh Ansh Ansh Ansh Ansh Ansh Ansh

Ansh Ansh Ansh Ansh

Ansh Ansh Ansh Ansh Ansh Ansh Ansh Ansh Ansh Ansh Ansh Ansh Ansh Ansh Ansh Ansh

Ansh Ansh Ansh Ansh Ansh Ansh Ansh Ansh Ansh Ansh Ansh Ansh Ansh Ansh Ansh Ansh

Ansh Ansh Ansh Ansh Ansh Ansh Ansh Ansh Ansh Ansh Ansh Ansh Ansh Ansh Ansh Ansh

Ansh Ansh Ansh Ansh Ansh Ansh Ansh Ansh Ansh Ansh Ansh Ansh Ansh Ansh Ansh Ansh

Ansh Ansh Ansh Ansh Ansh Ansh Ansh Ansh Ansh Ansh Ansh Ansh Ansh Ansh Ansh Ansh

Ansh Ansh Ansh Ansh Ansh Ansh Ansh Ansh Ansh Ansh Ansh Ansh Ansh Ansh Ansh Ansh

Ansh Ansh Ansh Ansh

Ansh Ansh Ansh Ansh Ansh Ansh Ansh Ansh Ansh Ansh Ansh Ansh Ansh Ansh Ansh Ansh

Ansh Ansh Ansh Ansh Ansh Ansh Ansh Ansh Ansh Ansh Ansh Ansh Ansh Ansh Ansh Ansh

Ansh Ansh Ansh Ansh Ansh Ansh Ansh Ansh Ansh Ansh Ansh Ansh Ansh Ansh Ansh Ansh

Ansh Ansh Ansh Ansh Ansh Ansh Ansh Ansh Ansh Ansh Ansh Ansh Ansh Ansh Ansh Ansh

Ansh Ansh Ansh Ansh Ansh Ansh Ansh Ansh Ansh Ansh Ansh Ansh Ansh Ansh Ansh Ansh

Ansh Ansh Ansh Ansh Ansh Ansh Ansh Ansh Ansh Ansh Ansh Ansh Ansh Ansh Ansh Ansh

Ansh Ansh Ansh Ansh

Ansh Ansh Ansh Ansh Ansh Ansh Ansh Ansh Ansh Ansh Ansh Ansh Ansh Ansh Ansh Ansh

Ansh Ansh Ansh Ansh Ansh Ansh Ansh Ansh Ansh Ansh Ansh Ansh Ansh Ansh Ansh Ansh

Ansh Ansh Ansh Ansh Ansh Ansh Ansh Ansh Ansh Ansh Ansh Ansh Ansh Ansh Ansh Ansh

Ansh Ansh Ansh Ansh Ansh Ansh Ansh Ansh Ansh Ansh Ansh Ansh Ansh Ansh Ansh Ansh

Ansh Ansh Ansh Ansh Ansh Ansh Ansh Ansh Ansh Ansh Ansh Ansh Ansh Ansh Ansh Ansh

Ansh Ansh Ansh Ansh Ansh Ansh Ansh Ansh Ansh Ansh Ansh Ansh Ansh Ansh Ansh Ansh

Ansh Ansh Ansh Ansh

Ansh Ansh Ansh Ansh Ansh Ansh Ansh Ansh Ansh Ansh Ansh Ansh Ansh Ansh Ansh Ansh

Ansh Ansh Ansh Ansh Ansh Ansh Ansh Ansh Ansh Ansh Ansh Ansh Ansh Ansh Ansh Ansh

Ansh Ansh Ansh Ansh Ansh Ansh Ansh Ansh Ansh Ansh Ansh Ansh Ansh Ansh Ansh Ansh

Ansh Ansh Ansh Ansh Ansh Ansh Ansh Ansh Ansh Ansh Ansh Ansh Ansh Ansh Ansh Ansh

Ansh Ansh Ansh Ansh Ansh Ansh Ansh Ansh Ansh Ansh Ansh Ansh Ansh Ansh Ansh Ansh

Ansh Ansh Ansh Ansh Ansh Ansh Ansh Ansh Ansh Ansh Ansh Ansh Ansh Ansh Ansh Ansh

Ansh Ansh Ansh Ansh

Ansh Ansh Ansh Ansh Ansh Ansh Ansh Ansh Ansh Ansh Ansh Ansh Ansh Ansh Ansh Ansh

Ansh Ansh Ansh Ansh Ansh Ansh Ansh Ansh Ansh Ansh Ansh Ansh Ansh Ansh Ansh Ansh

Ansh Ansh Ansh Ansh Ansh Ansh Ansh Ansh Ansh Ansh Ansh Ansh Ansh Ansh Ansh Ansh

Ansh Ansh Ansh Ansh Ansh Ansh Ansh Ansh Ansh Ansh Ansh Ansh Ansh Ansh Ansh Ansh

Ansh Ansh Ansh Ansh Ansh Ansh Ansh Ansh Ansh Ansh Ansh Ansh Ansh Ansh Ansh Ansh

Ansh Ansh Ansh Ansh Ansh Ansh Ansh Ansh Ansh Ansh Ansh Ansh Ansh Ansh Ansh Ansh

Ansh Ansh Ansh Ansh

Ansh Ansh Ansh Ansh Ansh Ansh Ansh Ansh Ansh Ansh Ansh Ansh Ansh Ansh Ansh Ansh

Ansh Ansh Ansh Ansh Ansh Ansh Ansh Ansh Ansh Ansh Ansh Ansh Ansh Ansh Ansh Ansh

Ansh Ansh Ansh Ansh Ansh Ansh Ansh Ansh Ansh Ansh Ansh Ansh Ansh Ansh Ansh Ansh

Ansh Ansh Ansh Ansh Ansh Ansh Ansh Ansh Ansh Ansh Ansh Ansh Ansh Ansh Ansh Ansh

Ansh Ansh Ansh Ansh Ansh Ansh Ansh Ansh Ansh Ansh Ansh Ansh Ansh Ansh Ansh Ansh

Ansh Ansh Ansh Ansh Ansh Ansh Ansh Ansh Ansh Ansh Ansh Ansh Ansh Ansh Ansh Ansh

Ansh Ansh Ansh Ansh

Ansh Ansh Ansh Ansh Ansh Ansh Ansh Ansh Ansh Ansh Ansh Ansh Ansh Ansh Ansh Ansh

Ansh Ansh Ansh Ansh Ansh Ansh Ansh Ansh Ansh Ansh Ansh Ansh Ansh Ansh Ansh Ansh

Ansh Ansh Ansh Ansh Ansh Ansh Ansh Ansh Ansh Ansh Ansh Ansh Ansh Ansh Ansh Ansh

Ansh Ansh Ansh Ansh Ansh Ansh Ansh Ansh Ansh Ansh Ansh Ansh Ansh Ansh Ansh Ansh

Ansh Ansh Ansh Ansh Ansh Ansh Ansh Ansh Ansh Ansh Ansh Ansh Ansh Ansh Ansh Ansh

Ansh Ansh Ansh Ansh Ansh Ansh Ansh Ansh Ansh Ansh Ansh Ansh Ansh Ansh Ansh Ansh

Ansh Ansh Ansh Ansh

Ansh Ansh Ansh Ansh Ansh Ansh Ansh Ansh Ansh Ansh Ansh Ansh Ansh Ansh Ansh Ansh

Ansh Ansh Ansh Ansh Ansh Ansh Ansh Ansh Ansh Ansh Ansh Ansh Ansh Ansh Ansh Ansh

Ansh Ansh Ansh Ansh Ansh Ansh Ansh Ansh Ansh Ansh Ansh Ansh Ansh Ansh Ansh Ansh

Ansh Ansh Ansh Ansh Ansh Ansh Ansh Ansh Ansh Ansh Ansh Ansh Ansh Ansh Ansh Ansh

Ansh Ansh Ansh Ansh Ansh Ansh Ansh Ansh Ansh Ansh Ansh Ansh Ansh Ansh Ansh Ansh

Ansh Ansh Ansh Ansh Ansh Ansh Ansh Ansh Ansh Ansh Ansh Ansh Ansh Ansh Ansh Ansh

Ansh Ansh Ansh Ansh

Ansh Ansh Ansh Ansh Ansh Ansh Ansh Ansh Ansh Ansh Ansh Ansh Ansh Ansh Ansh Ansh

Ansh Ansh Ansh Ansh Ansh Ansh Ansh Ansh Ansh Ansh Ansh Ansh Ansh Ansh Ansh Ansh

Ansh Ansh Ansh Ansh Ansh Ansh Ansh Ansh Ansh Ansh Ansh Ansh Ansh Ansh Ansh Ansh

Ansh Ansh Ansh Ansh Ansh Ansh Ansh Ansh Ansh Ansh Ansh Ansh Ansh Ansh Ansh Ansh

Ansh Ansh Ansh Ansh Ansh Ansh Ansh Ansh Ansh Ansh Ansh Ansh Ansh Ansh Ansh Ansh

Ansh Ansh Ansh Ansh Ansh Ansh Ansh Ansh Ansh Ansh Ansh Ansh Ansh Ansh Ansh Ansh

Ansh Ansh Ansh Ansh

Ansh Ansh Ansh Ansh Ansh Ansh Ansh Ansh Ansh Ansh Ansh Ansh Ansh Ansh Ansh Ansh

Ansh Ansh Ansh Ansh Ansh Ansh Ansh Ansh Ansh Ansh Ansh Ansh Ansh Ansh Ansh Ansh

Ansh Ansh Ansh Ansh Ansh Ansh Ansh Ansh Ansh Ansh Ansh Ansh Ansh Ansh Ansh Ansh

Ansh Ansh Ansh Ansh Ansh Ansh Ansh Ansh Ansh Ansh Ansh Ansh Ansh Ansh Ansh Ansh

Ansh Ansh Ansh Ansh Ansh Ansh Ansh Ansh Ansh Ansh Ansh Ansh Ansh Ansh Ansh Ansh

Ansh Ansh Ansh Ansh Ansh Ansh Ansh Ansh Ansh Ansh Ansh Ansh Ansh Ansh Ansh Ansh

Ansh Ansh Ansh Ansh

Ansh Ansh Ansh Ansh Ansh Ansh Ansh Ansh Ansh Ansh Ansh Ansh Ansh Ansh Ansh Ansh

Ansh Ansh Ansh Ansh Ansh Ansh Ansh Ansh Ansh Ansh Ansh Ansh Ansh Ansh Ansh Ansh

Ansh Ansh Ansh Ansh Ansh Ansh Ansh Ansh Ansh Ansh Ansh Ansh Ansh Ansh Ansh Ansh

Ansh Ansh Ansh Ansh Ansh Ansh Ansh Ansh Ansh Ansh Ansh Ansh Ansh Ansh Ansh Ansh

Ansh Ansh Ansh Ansh Ansh Ansh Ansh Ansh Ansh Ansh Ansh Ansh Ansh Ansh Ansh Ansh

Ansh Ansh Ansh Ansh Ansh Ansh Ansh Ansh Ansh Ansh Ansh Ansh Ansh Ansh Ansh Ansh

Ansh Ansh Ansh Ansh

Ansh Ansh Ansh Ansh Ansh Ansh Ansh Ansh Ansh Ansh Ansh Ansh Ansh Ansh Ansh Ansh

Ansh Ansh Ansh Ansh Ansh Ansh Ansh Ansh Ansh Ansh Ansh Ansh Ansh Ansh Ansh Ansh

Ansh Ansh Ansh Ansh Ansh Ansh Ansh Ansh Ansh Ansh Ansh Ansh Ansh Ansh Ansh Ansh

Ansh Ansh Ansh Ansh Ansh Ansh Ansh Ansh Ansh Ansh Ansh Ansh Ansh Ansh Ansh Ansh

Ansh Ansh Ansh Ansh Ansh Ansh Ansh Ansh Ansh Ansh Ansh Ansh Ansh Ansh Ansh Ansh

Ansh Ansh Ansh Ansh Ansh Ansh Ansh Ansh Ansh Ansh Ansh Ansh Ansh Ansh Ansh Ansh

Ansh Ansh Ansh Ansh

Ansh Ansh Ansh Ansh Ansh Ansh Ansh Ansh Ansh Ansh Ansh Ansh Ansh Ansh Ansh Ansh

Ansh Ansh Ansh Ansh Ansh Ansh Ansh Ansh Ansh Ansh Ansh Ansh Ansh Ansh Ansh Ansh

Ansh Ansh Ansh Ansh Ansh Ansh Ansh Ansh Ansh Ansh Ansh Ansh Ansh Ansh Ansh Ansh

Ansh Ansh Ansh Ansh Ansh Ansh Ansh Ansh Ansh Ansh Ansh Ansh Ansh Ansh Ansh Ansh

Ansh Ansh Ansh Ansh Ansh Ansh Ansh Ansh Ansh Ansh Ansh Ansh Ansh Ansh Ansh Ansh

Ansh Ansh Ansh Ansh Ansh Ansh Ansh Ansh Ansh Ansh Ansh Ansh Ansh Ansh Ansh Ansh

Ansh Ansh Ansh Ansh

Ansh Ansh Ansh Ansh Ansh Ansh Ansh Ansh Ansh Ansh Ansh Ansh Ansh Ansh Ansh Ansh

Ansh Ansh Ansh Ansh Ansh Ansh Ansh Ansh Ansh Ansh Ansh Ansh Ansh Ansh Ansh Ansh

Ansh Ansh Ansh Ansh Ansh Ansh Ansh Ansh Ansh Ansh Ansh Ansh Ansh Ansh Ansh Ansh

Ansh Ansh Ansh Ansh Ansh Ansh Ansh Ansh Ansh Ansh Ansh Ansh Ansh Ansh Ansh Ansh

Ansh Ansh Ansh Ansh Ansh Ansh Ansh Ansh Ansh Ansh Ansh Ansh Ansh Ansh Ansh Ansh

Ansh Ansh Ansh Ansh Ansh Ansh Ansh Ansh Ansh Ansh Ansh Ansh Ansh Ansh Ansh Ansh

Ansh Ansh Ansh Ansh

Ansh Ansh Ansh Ansh Ansh Ansh Ansh Ansh Ansh Ansh Ansh Ansh Ansh Ansh Ansh Ansh

Ansh Ansh Ansh Ansh Ansh Ansh Ansh Ansh Ansh Ansh Ansh Ansh Ansh Ansh Ansh Ansh

Ansh Ansh Ansh Ansh Ansh Ansh Ansh Ansh Ansh Ansh Ansh Ansh Ansh Ansh Ansh Ansh

Ansh Ansh Ansh Ansh Ansh Ansh Ansh Ansh Ansh Ansh Ansh Ansh Ansh Ansh Ansh Ansh

Ansh Ansh Ansh Ansh Ansh Ansh Ansh Ansh Ansh Ansh Ansh Ansh Ansh Ansh Ansh Ansh

Ansh Ansh Ansh Ansh Ansh Ansh Ansh Ansh Ansh Ansh Ansh Ansh Ansh Ansh Ansh Ansh

Ansh Ansh Ansh Ansh

Ansh Ansh Ansh Ansh Ansh Ansh Ansh Ansh Ansh Ansh Ansh Ansh Ansh Ansh Ansh Ansh

Ansh Ansh Ansh Ansh Ansh Ansh Ansh Ansh Ansh Ansh Ansh Ansh Ansh Ansh Ansh Ansh

Ansh Ansh Ansh Ansh Ansh Ansh Ansh Ansh Ansh Ansh Ansh Ansh Ansh Ansh Ansh Ansh

Ansh Ansh Ansh Ansh Ansh Ansh Ansh Ansh Ansh Ansh Ansh Ansh Ansh Ansh Ansh Ansh

Ansh Ansh Ansh Ansh Ansh Ansh Ansh Ansh Ansh Ansh Ansh Ansh Ansh Ansh Ansh Ansh

Ansh Ansh Ansh Ansh Ansh Ansh Ansh Ansh Ansh Ansh Ansh Ansh Ansh Ansh Ansh Ansh

Ansh Ansh Ansh Ansh

Ansh Ansh Ansh Ansh Ansh Ansh Ansh Ansh Ansh Ansh Ansh Ansh Ansh Ansh Ansh Ansh

Ansh Ansh Ansh Ansh Ansh Ansh Ansh Ansh Ansh Ansh Ansh Ansh Ansh Ansh Ansh Ansh

Ansh Ansh Ansh Ansh Ansh Ansh Ansh Ansh Ansh Ansh Ansh Ansh Ansh Ansh Ansh Ansh

Ansh Ansh Ansh Ansh Ansh Ansh Ansh Ansh Ansh Ansh Ansh Ansh Ansh Ansh Ansh Ansh

Ansh Ansh Ansh Ansh Ansh Ansh Ansh Ansh Ansh Ansh Ansh Ansh Ansh Ansh Ansh Ansh

Ansh Ansh Ansh Ansh Ansh Ansh Ansh Ansh Ansh Ansh Ansh Ansh Ansh Ansh Ansh Ansh

Ansh Ansh Ansh Ansh

Ansh Ansh Ansh Ansh Ansh Ansh Ansh Ansh Ansh Ansh Ansh Ansh Ansh Ansh Ansh Ansh

Ansh Ansh Ansh Ansh Ansh Ansh Ansh Ansh Ansh Ansh Ansh Ansh Ansh Ansh Ansh Ansh

Ansh Ansh Ansh Ansh Ansh Ansh Ansh Ansh Ansh Ansh Ansh Ansh Ansh Ansh Ansh Ansh

Ansh Ansh Ansh Ansh Ansh Ansh Ansh Ansh Ansh Ansh Ansh Ansh Ansh Ansh Ansh Ansh

Ansh Ansh Ansh Ansh Ansh Ansh Ansh Ansh Ansh Ansh Ansh Ansh Ansh Ansh Ansh Ansh

Ansh Ansh Ansh Ansh Ansh Ansh Ansh Ansh Ansh Ansh Ansh Ansh Ansh Ansh Ansh Ansh

Ansh Ansh Ansh Ansh

Ansh Ansh Ansh Ansh Ansh Ansh Ansh Ansh Ansh Ansh Ansh Ansh Ansh Ansh Ansh Ansh

Ansh Ansh Ansh Ansh Ansh Ansh Ansh Ansh Ansh Ansh Ansh Ansh Ansh Ansh Ansh Ansh

Ansh Ansh Ansh Ansh Ansh Ansh Ansh Ansh Ansh Ansh Ansh Ansh Ansh Ansh Ansh Ansh

Ansh Ansh Ansh Ansh Ansh Ansh Ansh Ansh Ansh Ansh Ansh Ansh Ansh Ansh Ansh Ansh

Ansh Ansh Ansh Ansh Ansh Ansh Ansh Ansh Ansh Ansh Ansh Ansh Ansh Ansh Ansh Ansh

Ansh Ansh Ansh Ansh Ansh Ansh Ansh Ansh Ansh Ansh Ansh Ansh Ansh Ansh Ansh Ansh

Ansh Ansh Ansh Ansh

Ansh Ansh Ansh Ansh Ansh Ansh Ansh Ansh Ansh Ansh Ansh Ansh Ansh Ansh Ansh Ansh

Ansh Ansh Ansh Ansh Ansh Ansh Ansh Ansh Ansh Ansh Ansh Ansh Ansh Ansh Ansh Ansh

Ansh Ansh Ansh Ansh Ansh Ansh Ansh Ansh Ansh Ansh Ansh Ansh Ansh Ansh Ansh Ansh

Ansh Ansh Ansh Ansh Ansh Ansh Ansh Ansh Ansh Ansh Ansh Ansh Ansh Ansh Ansh Ansh

Ansh Ansh Ansh Ansh Ansh Ansh Ansh Ansh Ansh Ansh Ansh Ansh Ansh Ansh Ansh Ansh

Ansh Ansh Ansh Ansh Ansh Ansh Ansh Ansh Ansh Ansh Ansh Ansh Ansh Ansh Ansh Ansh

Ansh Ansh Ansh Ansh

Ansh Ansh Ansh Ansh Ansh Ansh Ansh Ansh Ansh Ansh Ansh Ansh Ansh Ansh Ansh Ansh

Ansh Ansh Ansh Ansh Ansh Ansh Ansh Ansh Ansh Ansh Ansh Ansh Ansh Ansh Ansh Ansh

Ansh Ansh Ansh Ansh Ansh Ansh Ansh Ansh Ansh Ansh Ansh Ansh Ansh Ansh Ansh Ansh

Ansh Ansh Ansh Ansh Ansh Ansh Ansh Ansh Ansh Ansh Ansh Ansh Ansh Ansh Ansh Ansh

Ansh Ansh Ansh Ansh Ansh Ansh Ansh Ansh Ansh Ansh Ansh Ansh Ansh Ansh Ansh Ansh

Ansh Ansh Ansh Ansh Ansh Ansh Ansh Ansh Ansh Ansh Ansh Ansh Ansh Ansh Ansh Ansh

Ansh Ansh Ansh Ansh

Ansh Ansh Ansh Ansh Ansh Ansh Ansh Ansh Ansh Ansh Ansh Ansh Ansh Ansh Ansh Ansh

Ansh Ansh Ansh Ansh Ansh Ansh Ansh Ansh Ansh Ansh Ansh Ansh Ansh Ansh Ansh Ansh

Ansh Ansh Ansh Ansh Ansh Ansh Ansh Ansh Ansh Ansh Ansh Ansh Ansh Ansh Ansh Ansh

Ansh Ansh Ansh Ansh Ansh Ansh Ansh Ansh Ansh Ansh Ansh Ansh Ansh Ansh Ansh Ansh

Ansh Ansh Ansh Ansh Ansh Ansh Ansh Ansh Ansh Ansh Ansh Ansh Ansh Ansh Ansh Ansh

Ansh Ansh Ansh Ansh Ansh Ansh Ansh Ansh Ansh Ansh Ansh Ansh Ansh Ansh Ansh Ansh

Ansh Ansh Ansh Ansh

Ansh Ansh Ansh Ansh Ansh Ansh Ansh Ansh Ansh Ansh Ansh Ansh Ansh Ansh Ansh Ansh

Ansh Ansh Ansh Ansh Ansh Ansh Ansh Ansh Ansh Ansh Ansh Ansh Ansh Ansh Ansh Ansh

Ansh Ansh Ansh Ansh Ansh Ansh Ansh Ansh Ansh Ansh Ansh Ansh Ansh Ansh Ansh Ansh

Ansh Ansh Ansh Ansh Ansh Ansh Ansh Ansh Ansh Ansh Ansh Ansh Ansh Ansh Ansh Ansh

Ansh Ansh Ansh Ansh Ansh Ansh Ansh Ansh Ansh Ansh Ansh Ansh Ansh Ansh Ansh Ansh

Ansh Ansh Ansh Ansh Ansh Ansh Ansh Ansh Ansh Ansh Ansh Ansh Ansh Ansh Ansh Ansh

Ansh Ansh Ansh Ansh

Ansh Ansh Ansh Ansh Ansh Ansh Ansh Ansh Ansh Ansh Ansh Ansh Ansh Ansh Ansh Ansh

Ansh Ansh Ansh Ansh Ansh Ansh Ansh Ansh Ansh Ansh Ansh Ansh Ansh Ansh Ansh Ansh

Ansh Ansh Ansh Ansh Ansh Ansh Ansh Ansh Ansh Ansh Ansh Ansh Ansh Ansh Ansh Ansh

Ansh Ansh Ansh Ansh Ansh Ansh Ansh Ansh Ansh Ansh Ansh Ansh Ansh Ansh Ansh Ansh

Ansh Ansh Ansh Ansh Ansh Ansh Ansh Ansh Ansh Ansh Ansh Ansh Ansh Ansh Ansh Ansh

Ansh Ansh Ansh Ansh Ansh Ansh Ansh Ansh Ansh Ansh Ansh Ansh Ansh Ansh Ansh Ansh

Ansh Ansh Ansh Ansh

Ansh Ansh Ansh Ansh Ansh Ansh Ansh Ansh Ansh Ansh Ansh Ansh Ansh Ansh Ansh Ansh

Ansh Ansh Ansh Ansh Ansh Ansh Ansh Ansh Ansh Ansh Ansh Ansh Ansh Ansh Ansh Ansh

Ansh Ansh Ansh Ansh Ansh Ansh Ansh Ansh Ansh Ansh Ansh Ansh Ansh Ansh Ansh Ansh

Ansh Ansh Ansh Ansh Ansh Ansh Ansh Ansh Ansh Ansh Ansh Ansh Ansh Ansh Ansh Ansh

Ansh Ansh Ansh Ansh Ansh Ansh Ansh Ansh Ansh Ansh Ansh Ansh Ansh Ansh Ansh Ansh

Ansh Ansh Ansh Ansh Ansh Ansh Ansh Ansh Ansh Ansh Ansh Ansh Ansh Ansh Ansh Ansh

Ansh Ansh Ansh Ansh

Thank you ansh for all the memorable moments in my life.

9 798889 751984

Printed by Libri Plureos GmbH in Hamburg,
Germany